A Killer

Missteps

A Killer Missteps

A Luca Mystery Book 8

Dan Petrosini

Other Books by Dan

Acknowledgments

Special thanks to Julie, Stephanie and Jennifer for their love and support, and thanks to Squad Sergeant Craig Perrilli for his counsel on the real world of law enforcement. He helps me keep it real.

Chapter 1

Our home phone rang. I looked at Mary Ann and put my coffee down. She said, "Don't answer it. Somebody calling this early, it has to be a sales call."

The only people who called the house line were spammers. The office occasionally would if I didn't answer my cell. My phone didn't show a missed call, but I still went to get it. I had to.

An unsettled feeling had descended on me a day ago. As I'd gotten older, my antennae had become sharper. It wasn't a belief in a mystical power to predict or detect something, but my cumulative experience signaled that something was about to happen.

"Hello."

It was an internet call. As soon as I heard the way my name was butchered, I said no thank you and hung up.

"Who was it?"

"A sales call."

"Told you. You know, you're like a caged tiger."

I shrugged and sipped my coffee.

"If something is going to happen, Frank, you'll deal with it when it does."

I nibbled on the crust I'd cut away from Jessie's toast. Being a homicide detective was the opposite of fatherhood. While I was on the job, I was dealing with the aftermath of a violent act. It was reactionary. Being a parent was preparatory. We took steps to make sure Jessie was safe, healthy, and behaved properly. We were molding a life.

I didn't want to tell Mary Ann this feeling was different than past ones. My first hope was that it didn't involve Jessie or Mary Ann. I couldn't bear anything happening to them. My other concern was that my cancer would resurface.

I kissed Jessie. "I'm going to head into the office."

"Okay. As soon as Frannie gets here, I'm leaving as well."

Our neighbor was filling in since the nanny we settled on had pulled out at the last minute, and we couldn't agree on who to hire next. "She should be here already. If she doesn't come or wants to send a sub, don't go in. We don't know who they are. I'll come home."

"Oh boy, Frank. You can be so dramatic."

***

Derrick was on the phone. I took my jacket off and picked up the coffee he'd brought me. Derrick hung up.

"We have a body."

"I knew it."

"What?"

"Nothing. Who is it?"

"Thirty-five-year-old female, Jill Evans. Ex-husband found her and called nine one one."

"Where?"

"Her house, out in Lely, on St. Andrews Boulevard."

"Tell them not to touch anything."

"Mackenzie is out there. He's good; we'll be okay."

I grabbed my coffee. "Let's get moving."

We hopped in the Cherokee with Derrick behind the wheel. I sent a text to Mary Ann telling her we had a corpse. I wanted her to know it wasn't drama; it was life.

We took Santa Barbara Boulevard until it ended at Rattlesnake Hammock Road, turning into St. Andrew's Boulevard. Golden letters on a wall announced it as Lely Country Club.

"I thought Lely was gated."

"Me too. Maybe parts of it are. Dispatch mentioned something like Lely Palms."

We drove past a short stretch of multifamily units toward the flashing lights of two patrol cars and an ambulance.

They were parked in front of a well-maintained one-story home. A white Ford Taurus was in the driveway. Standing by the garage door were a uniformed officer and a man in a golf shirt.

I opened the car door and heard crying. Across the street four woman were huddled together. Heads down, we ducked under the yellow police tape and signed in with the officer guarding the scene.

The gatekeeper pointed to the garage. "That's the husband, or ex-husband, as I understand it. He's the one who called it in. You want to talk to him?"

"Not yet. We need to see the scene."

"Binino is inside. He'll fill you in. We're going to let the EMT guys go, okay?"

Nodding, we put booties on and stepped into the foyer. Its white tile ran throughout the house.

"Hey, Luca, Derrick."

I pulled out a pair of gloves. "How's it going, Charlie?"

"All right. You?"

"Not bad. Anybody touch anything?"

"No. I got here first. The husband was here, but that's it. I kept him inside until the other guys arrived."

"That's the way to do it. What do we have here?"

"Female Caucasian, Jill Evans. She's in the kitchen."

I turned into the kitchen. A pair of bare feet extended past a small island. Jill Evans was a small woman. She was on her back. Her pink T-shirt was hiked up, revealing an outie belly button. The top button of her clam digger jeans was open.

Her brown hair was a mess of tangles. It appeared that a struggle had taken place.

A checked towel was on the floor, and a new pod of Eight O'Clock coffee had rolled against the cabinetry's kickboard. A box of Raisin Bran was on its side next to a clean bowl, no spoon in sight.

To the right of the body was a white COACH handbag. Its purse was two feet away. It didn't contain any cash or credit cards. Was she killed in a robbery? Or had the murderer attempted to stage this poor woman's death?

I took a long look at the body before crouching. I pointed to her neck.

"See here, Derrick; pressure was applied."

"Yeah, I see the marks. She was strangled to death."

"There doesn't seem to be a wound of any kind, but we can't be sure. Maybe she was poisoned and clutched her throat in reaction."

I looked at her hands, no markings. "We'll see what forensics can tell us. Meanwhile, let's go over this house, and see what we can turn up."

We went room by room. It looked like a normal day unfolding: bed unmade, toothbrush wet, yesterday's clothing on the closet floor. A family room end table had half a glass of lukewarm water on it and yesterday's newspaper.

None of the windows were unlocked. The open slider to the lanai was a puzzle. Was that how the killer got in? We needed to know.

"Let's see what the husband has to say."

"This should be interesting."

"Let me do the talking. You take down what he says. We're going to need to document this, especially if he's involved in her death."

Chapter 2

His hand had the structure of a towel.

"We're sorry for your loss, sir, but we have a couple of questions that can't wait."

George Evans was wiry with sandy hair that was thinning. His lips were nonexistent. It was a difficult time for him, but I couldn't help thinking he looked like the type of man who rarely smiled.

"I understand."

"Tell us what happened."

"Well, I don't know what happened. I came here—"

"What time was that?"

"Just before ten o'clock."

Out of the corner of my eye I saw Gianelli coming up the driveway. He had two cameras slung over his shoulder. I nodded at him. He winked in return. We'd worked a dozen homicides together. He was a pro; I didn't need to hold his hand.

"Okay. Go on."

"I rang the bell, but Jill didn't answer. I tried again and started to get worried something was wrong. So, I went around back to see if she was there. She wasn't, and I went through the screen door onto the lanai. A slider was open."

With temperatures in the high seventies and zero humidity in the first week of March, it wasn't unusual for doors and windows to be open.

"Did she normally leave the slider open?"

"Jill didn't like air-conditioning, so yeah, as long as the humidity wasn't bad."

"Did you notice anything unusual?"

"No, but I didn't look around much. I just called her name and walked in. And then, then I saw her." He hung his head. "She was lying there, and I couldn't process what I was seeing. I didn't know what to do."

"Of course. What did you do next?"

"I shouted for her to get up, and, and then I shook her, but she wasn't responding. I tried to take her pulse, but she didn't seem to be breathing. I was going to give her mouth to mouth, but I never did it before, and I figured I should call nine one one first."

"Is that when you called nine one one?"

"Yes, I tried to tell them what was going on, and they said to give her mouth to mouth and walked me through it. But I wasn't sure I was doing it right, and it wasn't working. Then they said to press up and down on her chest to try to get her heart pumping again. But nothing worked."

"What did you do next?"

"I ran outside for help. To find somebody. Somebody who knew how to do it right because I was doing it wrong."

"Did anyone assist you?"

"Nobody was outside, so I went back in, hoping maybe she'd woken up."

"And after you went back inside?"

"I heard the sirens and knew help was coming, so I went out to wait for them. But when they came, they tried but said they couldn't do anything for her, that she was gone . . ."

"Let's go back to when you arrived. You rang the bell, right?"

"Yeah, but she never answered."

"And when she didn't come to the door, you said you became worried. What gave you the impression something could be wrong?"

"I, I don't know. I just felt it."

He was a prime suspect. I couldn't tell him about my premonitions. "Something had to make you feel that way. You only rang the bell once. She could've been in the bathroom or busy."

"It's just something I felt, that's all. We were married for four years. I knew Jill inside out."

"I understand the two of you divorced."

"Yes, but we were getting back together."

"Why did you come here today?"

"Jill called me. She said she had something to talk to me about."

"What do you think it was about?"

"I don't know."

"Are you sure? You were married four years and said you were getting back together. You had to know something."

"No, really, I had no idea."

"When did she call?"

"Last night, around dinnertime."

"So it was nothing urgent."

"No, she said she just wanted to talk."

"You said earlier that you knew something was wrong, and when I asked about it you said you knew her inside and out. Did I get that right, Derrick?"

"He said, 'We were married for four years. I knew Jill inside out.'"

"So, what did you think, or what feeling did you get about what she wanted to talk about?"

"I swear I don't know. She didn't say much when she called. To tell you the truth, I didn't like it. She was secretive, if you know what I mean. I felt like it was going to be bad news or something."

Swearing and saying you were telling the truth in one sentence—my skeptic alarm rang so loud I thought the fire department might be on the way.

"And when you got here, she didn't say anything?"

"What are you talking about? She was unconscious, on the floor."

It was worth a shot. "What do you think happened to her?"

"She was attacked, probably that bastard Jafar. He was jealous of us getting back together."

"Who is that?"

"Jafar Kapur, he was practically living with Jill. Young punk is what he is. He thinks he's some kind of tech wizard. He even wears those stupid Google glasses. Can you imagine?"

Derrick asked for the proper spelling of the boyfriend's name, and I asked, "This man Jafar, do you know where he works?"

"Off Old Forty-One, in the technology park. He's got some start-up thing going there about life extension. It's a bunch of bullshit, if you ask me."

I remembered reading something in the paper about it. Who knew if the attempt to extend people's lives was nonsense or not, but I was rooting for the venture to succeed.

"And where do you work?"

"Cool Zone on J and C Boulevard. I used to have my own HVAC company, but I ran into a rough patch and had to shut it down."

The forensics van pulled up. Derrick took George Evans' contact details, and I went to talk with the technicians. We had two crews, and both were methodical. As they were putting their coveralls on, a white Buick SUV pulled up. It was Dr. Bilotti, the county coroner.

Chapter 3

"Hello, Frank. I was thinking of you last night. I had an incredible Amarone."

"That the one you told me about at Ferguson's retirement party? The one that tastes like raisins?"

"So, you were listening. A lot of the flavor profile comes from the fact that after they pick the grapes, they dry them out on mats under the sun. Then, when they're all shriveled up, they press them for the juice."

He was moving stiffly. Either his back was bothering him, or he was catching rigor mortis from the corpses he worked with.

"That's interesting. I have to pick up a bottle or two."

He took two bags out of his trunk. "If I remember, I'll bring one in for you."

"That's not necessary, but I won't turn a bottle down."

"Heard this one isn't messy."

"Could be a strangulation, but you're the pro. The husband found her—"

"No more, please. I don't want my judgment colored."

Dr. Bilotti was a great guy off the job, but he moved slower than a slug. Just watching him put his gloves on was enough to make my heart race. Gianelli looked at me and rolled his eyes as Bilotti moved his head over the crime scene at half the speed of a lawn sprinkler.

The coroner knelt by the body and shined his penlight into each eye. There was no life. Bilotti inserted an ear thermometer and recorded the temperature of each ear. He noted the time and the clothing on the body.

"Doc, I photographed the body and the room with a wide angle and took overlapping shots before doing close-ups. I repeated it, centering the body. I took two hundred and eighty stills before using video."

"Good work."

"Do you need me for anything else?"

We both knew the answer. "I'd appreciate you sticking around a little longer, and I need somebody to get a thermostat reading."

Bilotti took out a pad and began sketching the crime scene. Holding his laser measuring device, he began noting the distances between the body and the corners of the room. Then he started jotting down how far the corpse was from the counters and kitchen table. He was just getting started; I knew I had time.

"Doc, I need to use the restroom."

He turned around. His look turned me into a ten-year-old in front of the school principal. "If you must. Gianelli, photograph the facilities before he uses them."

I sent a text to Mary Ann to let her know I'd be late for dinner as Gianelli photographed a powder room in need of updating.

Two hours later, my lower back was aching as Bilotti took another look around. "The body can be removed. But nothing else is to be disturbed."

"Looks like she met her attacker around here, and there was a struggle."

"You're on the right path, Frank. I'll formalize my findings as soon as possible."

"It was strangulation, right?"

"On the surface, that is how it appears. The autopsy will confirm it."

***

"This is an easy call, Derrick. Have the entire property taped off. This place is a crime scene. Put in a request for a twenty-four-seven guard. I don't want the killer or a nosy neighbor getting access."

"Got it."

"Make sure the uniforms know, and don't let them leave until everything is secure and a guard posted."

"Okay. When you were with Bilotti, I put a call into emergency services. They're sending over the nine-one-one audio files."

"Good thinking."

"They said there were two calls."

"Two?"

"Yeah, first one was terminated immediately, and the second came in eighteen minutes later."

"From the same phone?"

"Yes, one registered to Jill Evans."

"Interesting. You know what? Tell Ferguson to stay here, and make sure the scene is secure. You and I need to go over the audio together."

***

Derrick closed the door to our office and rolled his chair to my desk. I opened the email with the 911 calls. Both originated from 540-400-1732, a Virginia area code registered to Jillian Evans.

The first call came in at 9:49 a.m. I clicked on play.

"This is nine one one. What's your emergency?"

I kept my eyes on the voice graph. No movement.

"What's your emergency?"

Click.

"You think he was having second thoughts, Frank?"

"Could be. He may have wanted to get his story straight. Let's see what he actually says."

The second call was made at 10:07, eighteen minutes after the first call.

"This is nine one one. What's your emergency?"

"My wife, she needs help."

"What is the address?"

"Six three one seven St. Andrews Boulevard. Hurry! She's not breathing."

"An ambulance is on the way, sir. Open her mouth; check for any obstructions."

"There isn't any. Please help me."

"Let's try giving her mouth-to-mouth CPR. Do you know how to do that?"

"I tried. It didn't work."

"Let's try again. Put your mouth over her mouth, pinch the nose shut. Breathe into her mouth. Repeat. Again. Observe her chest. Is there any movement?"

"No! She's not breathing."

"Stay calm, sir. Help is on the way. I'd like you to try chest compressions."

The 911 operator walked Evans through the procedure.

"It's not working. Please, you have to help me."

"Stay calm. Help is on the way."

Click.

Derrick said, "He sounded pretty frazzled to me."

"Either that, or he used the time between calls to rehearse."

"Be tough to do that. He had no idea what the operator was going to say."

"Maybe, but you watch enough cop shows, and you'll have a pretty good idea."

"True. He didn't cry on the call."

"We don't know anything about him. If we find out he cries easily, then we have a frame of reference."

"If he did it, why didn't he run?"

"It could be another calculation. He knew he'd be a suspect. If he takes off, he'd have to worry about who saw him there that morning. Remember, there's no shortage of people who think they can fool us."

"Maybe the voice graph can tell us something."

"It'd be nice, but it's less reliable than a polygraph. Once the autopsy is done, we'll get a time of death, and see what else pops up."

Chapter 4

Doctor Bilotti moved his arms robotlike as he said, "It is my finding that Jillian Evans was a victim of strangulation. There is no evidence that a ligature of any kind was used. This was a manual strangulation, using hands."

"Male hands?"

"It's difficult to be certain. The victim is a small woman, and a large amount of force wasn't necessary. But given the overwhelming majority of female victims at the hands of a male, it would be safe assumption."

"But she was definitely strangled."

"Obstruction of the carotid arteries and jugular veins resulted in her death. The cessation of oxygenation leads to anoxic encephalopathy; the brain dies from a lack of oxygen. Petechiae, in the form of two minuscule dots, were found on both facial cheeks."

"Pitee what?"

"Petechiae, markings from broken capillaries."

"What about a time of death?"

"Between nine and ten a.m."

"How certain are you?"

"Beginning signs of livor mortis—"

"Pooling of blood in the body?"

"Exactly. Between that and the corpse's body temperature, I'm confident death occurred between the hours of nine to ten a.m."

"Good. Any signs of sexual assault?"

"No, but evidence shows the victim recently had intercourse."

"The night before?"

"Within the last two to three days."

"Can you narrow it down further?"

"Not unless I knew how long the male was able to forestall a climax."

"Anything in her system?"

"The first set of blood panels will be back from the lab in a day or two."

"What else you can tell me that would help?"

"Either the victim was taken by surprise from the rear, or she had her arms pinned down while the strangulation was unfolding."

"What makes you say that?"

"I didn't find anything under any of her fingernails. Excepting in cases where a choke hold is used to cause carotid obstruction, resulting in death in fifteen seconds, a victim will claw at the attacker's hands, attempting to relieve the pressure."

"Do you believe it was a choke hold that killed her?"

"I don't believe so, but it is in the realm of possibilities."

"Thanks, Doc. Let me know when the toxicology reports came back."

Going back to my office, I pondered the time of death. Bilotti pinned it between 9 and 10 a.m. There was some wiggle room in it, but it lined up with 911 calls made by her ex-husband, George Evans. From the outset, the likelihood it was him was high—no, it was stratospheric.

***

It was the first homicide involving strangulation since I'd moved to paradise.

"We were overdue for one, Derrick."

"A murder?"

"No, a strangulation case. One in every nine violent deaths is by suffocation or strangling, and it's especially common in domestic violence cases."

"That's probably what we have here. The husband is suspect number one. By the way, phone records confirm she called him the night before like he said."

"Okay. But we can't discount the possibility of a robbery. Bilotti said there were no signs of sexual assault, so if it wasn't a break-in or walk-in, it had to be someone she knew."

"St. Andrews is a busy road. If it was a robbery, someone had to see something."

"The time of day fits with a burglary. Thieves like to operate when no one is home, and it could be they figured the house was empty. They gain access through the lanai, enter the house and encounter her. She begins to scream, and they silence her."

"We'll canvass the neighborhood to see if any of the neighbors might have heard something."

"If they did, they should have called it in. Either they weren't home, or the road noise from Rattlesnake Hammock Road obscured it." I pointed to the map taped to the whiteboard. "No homes back up to her side of the street. It's all preserve."

"I'll check with the landscapers and pool guys."

"Check with the county; see if any meter readers or inspectors were in the area. And garbage pickup, I didn't see any cans out that day, but double-check it."

"You think someone could have walked over from the back of Manor Care Health?"

"At this point, if some kind of robbery is involved, we have to look at every possible place they could have come from. I don't see them parking in the driveway and ringing the bell."

Chapter 5

I pulled into the technology park on Old 41 and circled to Building C. A large, orange sign with an offbeat font read Xtended Living. It looked like something that should have been in Silicon Valley. Not that I'd ever been to California.

Workstations, each with two monitors, covered the entire space. The music playing was loud and by Garth Brooks. More people here had tattoos than at Fort Myers Beach on a weekend.

I recognized Jafar Kapur from his driver's license photo. He was talking to a kid with a neon-green slug in his earlobe. Jafar knew I was coming, and with my sports jacket, he didn't need to be an internet whiz kid to know who I was. Jafar smiled and waved me in. We went into his office, which was small and messy.

Thin, Jafar's teeth were LED-like.

"Welcome to Xtended Living, Detective."

His right index finger was clipped at the first knuckle. "I read about this in the paper. It's a fascinating idea, and believe me, for my sake, I hope you hit it out of the park."

"For decades, the scientific community has been focused on treating disease, illness, and keeping people healthy. I wondered why so few efforts were being made in the longevity field. I'm convinced that if we focus on why someone lives to a hundred and fifteen, we can identify and amplify those traits."

"How far away are you?"

"We have already identified microbes and polyphenols that help and are easy to adapt through a dietary regime, and if people would get regular exercise, simply walking instead of driving at times, they could add years to their lives."

Mary Ann was right, I needed to lose weight. Maybe I could get a bicycle. "We'll have to figure out how to pay for longer retirements."

"Yes. The work we are doing on telomeres is incredibly promising. If it goes the way I believe it will, people will be working into their late eighties."

I hoped Jafar had nothing to do with the murder of Jillian Evans; we needed him.

"I have no idea what telomeres are, but it sounds fascinating. I'd like to continue this, but I have some questions concerning Jillian Evans."

His sunny disposition crumbled. "I can't believe what happened. It feels surreal."

"I'm sorry for your loss, Mr. Kapur. How long did you know her?"

"A bit less than two years. She was separated from her husband, and one day she was struggling to load her car with a case of water at the supermarket. I helped her, and we hit it off, like it was meant to be. It was so unexpected but natural."

"I understand you were essentially living together."

"I still have a home, but we spent most of our time together."

"Where is your house?"

"Spanish Wells. I walk back and forth from here when I'm there. It's just over two miles away."

This guy was shaming me. "What about her husband, George Evans? He claims they were in the midst of a reconciliation."

He shook his head. "He was no good for her. He couldn't provide for her financially and left her with a mountain of debt when his so-called business folded."

"Was he seeing her romantically?"

"Look, George didn't get it. He kept coming around, saying he needed to talk about this or that issue, or it was something about the divorce."

"Do you believe he could have done this to her?"

"Absolutely. Jill told me he became physically abusive with her when they were married. She said that was the primary reason she decided to leave him."

"When she said he became physical, can you expand upon that?"

"She didn't talk about it. As you can imagine, it was painful for her, but I know he struck her at least once."

"You're certain he struck her?"

"Absolutely."

"Is there anything else you can tell me about George Evans?"

"I didn't know him other than through Jill. He didn't like me, and I get it, but he was dark, a negative person. Not a good one to be around."

"Where were you the morning of March fifth?"

"Right here. I left Jill's house at eight."

"And you came straight here?"

"Yes, but I did get my café mocha from the Starbucks by her house. I can't function without one. I don't know where'd we be without caffeine."

"I need a good two cups to get moving."

"Caffeine has other benefits besides acting as a stimulant. It contains many antioxidants and seems to help protect your brain from dementia."

What do you know, we have a miracle drug on our hands.

Chapter 6

Forensics had identified two distinct samples of DNA on Jillian Evans. They were both male. There were three hairs on the body that matched the DNA found on the neck of the victim and a second set of DNA belonging to another man, also on the neck.

It was my belief that the hair had to be from George Evans, the ex-husband. If not, it could be the killer's. According to the ex's account and following the instructions from the 911 technician, Evans had been over the body attempting to resuscitate the victim.

The DNA on the neck could have been from supporting the head or from strangling her. I couldn't see the husband resisting a request for a DNA swab. That would identify one batch of DNA. The question was, to whom did the other belong to? Most likely it was Jafar's, but we needed to be certain.

George Evans was the unofficial, number-one suspect. For more times than I cared to recall, it was a spouse killing their spouse. Overwhelmingly so when it was a female victim.

Then there were the 911 calls. Why two? Why eighteen minutes apart? Staring at the pictures on the whiteboard, I focused on George Evans. What could have happened? He went to the house, claiming she asked him to come talk. She had made a call to him, but we had no way to verify the content of the call. She could have told him to leave her alone. That is was over between them.

If she did summon him, he came without an agenda, open to hear what she had to say. What could she have said to provoke him into choking her? It probably revolved around their relationship, which was reigniting, according to him, or the ending of such.

She unloads whatever she had to say, and Evans strangles her, panicking when she becomes lifeless. He calls 911, immediately ending the call when he realizes he needs a plan.

What did he do in the eighteen minutes? That's a lifetime when you're with a dead body.

Evans used his ex-wife's phone to make the calls. They were the only ones made during the period from her phone. Had he used his phone to call someone? I made a note to request a log of his phone activity. Something I should have done already. I chalked it up to the effects of the chemo I'd been doused with a few years ago. I moved back to the strangulation.

George Evans claimed that he left the house during the time between calls to see if anyone could help him. Was that true panic or staged?

Two things at the crime scene needed explanation. The first was the open slider that led to the lanai. Was that the way the killer gained access? Or had the killer left that way, leaving it open to support the look of an intrusion?

The pocketbook on the floor and the empty purse could be evidence of a burglary or to disguise the crime as one. Clarifying whether we were looking at an insider or searching for an outsider would make a solve miles easier. We needed to start with the ex-husband.

George Evans had been the owner of a small HVAC business using the name of Keep Cool. It would be the height of irony if he turned out to be the one who lost it. I searched the state employee database and made a list of the five people who'd worked for it.

***

It was just after eleven. She'd never expect me at this hour. It was either my immaturity or law enforcement training, but I loved surprising people. I pulled in the driveway and went through the front door.

Jimena Cruz peered over her reading glasses. No smile, no hello, just an impervious stare before she went back to knitting. Jessie was sleeping on a Sesame Street play blanket near the sliders.

I waved and ducked into the den. Pulling open a drawer, I counted to ten and closed it before going back into the family room.

Jimena's eyes followed me. As I tiptoed toward Jessie, she cleared her throat as a warning. How was it that I was uncomfortable in my own house? I backed off mumbling that I'd forgotten something in the house before slinking out the front door.

Not only did I dislike the idea of a stranger watching my daughter, I didn't like the lady doing it. She acted like it was her damn house. Did she discount me, knowing she really worked for Mary Ann?

The entire nanny process was causing friction between Mary Ann and me. After I vetoed two women she thought were perfect, she hired Jimena without consulting me.

Mary Ann was right. In my eyes, nobody was good enough to take care of Jessie. But I felt it was an egregious violation of our marriage for her to choose our daughter's caretaker alone.

We had a blowup, or I did anyway, and when she defended her decision, it made me madder. A week had passed since our argument, and we still weren't back to normal. I kept looking for any changes in Jessie, but thankfully, she was her beautiful self.

***

With Jessie in bed, we settled into our spots in the family room and put the tube on. I avoided putting *Jeopardy* on. It was my show. I put WINK news on instead. What a surprise, the weather was on. We had the most unbelievable weather in Southwest Florida, yet all the meteorologists droned on about this storm or the odds it would rain. It drove me nuts when they'd talk about a cold front, dropping to sixty in the middle of the night.

"Didn't they say it was supposed to rain today?"

Mary Ann looked up from her iPad. "They say that every day."

"You know why God created weathermen? To make economists look good."

I got her to smile.

"You okay?"

"I'm fine, Frank."

"Okay, you're just a bit quiet tonight."

"Did you come to spy on Jimena today?"

Shit. "Spy? What are you talking about?"

"Jimena said you came by around eleven today?"

"I forgot something in the office."

"You came in through the front door."

Sometimes being married to a cop made things difficult. "I thought Jessie might be sleeping, and the garage door might wake her."

"You scared Jimena."

"Is that why she didn't say a damn word to me? I mean, I feel like a frigging stranger in my own house."

"Maybe she senses your hostility toward her."

"Hostility? Come on, Mary Ann, don't you think she should make an effort?"

"You've been against the idea since day one. Get used to it. If you took the time to notice, you'd see that Jessica is developing a bond with her. Give the lady a chance, Frank."

She was right. I was hostile. Maybe I was taking it out on Jimena because I was mad at the entire idea and pissed at Mary Ann for going around me.

Chapter 7

A Crystal Clear truck was parked in front of 29 Avocado Street. We waited for Michael Borsky to finish servicing the pink home's pool. Contacting the pool companies that serviced the victim's street may have yielded some fruit.

A tall, twenty-something rolled a gear-filled cart to his truck.

"Michael Borsky?"

"Yep, that's me. You with the police?"

I held up my badge. "Detective Luca. I understand you may have seen something regarding the homicide on St. Andrews."

"That was terrible. I feel awful for that lady. She was nice. Always offered me water when I did her pool."

"What can you tell me about that day?"

"Well, I usually do the St. Andrews route on Fridays, but Mrs. Martin, she lives two houses down, she's a pain in the ass, always complaining her pool isn't clear. She called the office, not once but two times, saying she had algae growing. So, the boss, he sent me out to make a special trip."

"And you made that trip on Tuesday, March fifth?"

"Yep, and the pool didn't have any algae either. I think the old lady is losing it."

"What time were you at the Martin home?"

"It was around nine thirty in the morning."

"Are you sure?"

"Yeah, Tuesday is my lightest day. I went to the warehouse to get a powerful algae preventer, in case Mrs. Martin was right. It would be her first time. I loaded the truck and went straight to St. Andrews. It took a good twenty-five minutes to get to Lely."

"Where is the warehouse?

"Off Bernwood, in Bonita."

"Okay, you get to the Martin home, which is two doors from the Evans house, at nine thirty. What happened?"

"Well, the first thing I did was log into my tablet, to let the boss know I was there—"

"Your company has a program that tracks its service techs?"

"Yeah, they put it in about two years ago. Some of the guys are lazy asses and would sit in the truck for a half an hour. Made us all look bad."

"You're at the Martin house at nine thirty. You log in, then what?"

"I went around back to check out the pool. It looked pretty good to me. Mrs. Martin came out. I said hello and that I thought the water looked fine, but I'd add a large dose of algae killer just to be sure."

"Did she stay outside the house with you?"

"No. She said she was going to walk her dog."

"Tell me what happened next."

"I went to the truck to get a bottle of algaecide. It was really just a show for Mrs. Martin. I made sure she saw me taking the jug to the back. When I was pouring it in the pool, spilling some in as I circled the pool, I saw something moving in the back."

"In back of the Martin house?"

"No, kinda like angling away from the Evans house."

"From what direction?"

"Like going to Rattlesnake Hammock Road or that health care place."

"What did you see?"

"It was a guy back there. It looked like he was in a hurry."

"Was he running?"

"Kind of."

"Did you see his face?"

"No. I saw his back."

"What can you tell me about this man? What kind of a build?"

"I'd say he was medium built."

"Height?"

"Tough to say, but not short or tall."

"Hair color?"

"Brown, I think."

"What was he wearing?"

"Looked like it was maybe jeans, long pants, and a light-colored shirt."

After thanking him for stepping forward, I jumped into the Cherokee. It wasn't earth shattering, but it was a lead to follow. We needed to hit the pavement, and see what anyone else may have seen.

I sent Derrick a text to check with the pool company to verify the exact time Borsky arrived at the Martin house. I also asked him to identify the landscapers used in the neighborhood and find out the day and times they came by.

A text chimed in right after I hit send. It was from Dr. Bilotti asking me to call him.

"Hi, Doc, what's going on?"

"I received the blood panels on Jillian Evans."

"Any alcohol or illicit drugs?"

"No presence detected, and no poisons either."

"Okay, Doc, good try. I appreciate you letting me know."

"Hold on, I didn't know whether you were aware of it or not, but the victim was pregnant."

"Pregnant?"

"Indeed."

"How far along?"

"I can't be certain, but it was early."

"We need to know who the father is."

"The body has been released to the mother."

What did this mean? Who was the father? The boyfriend, the ex-husband, or someone else? If the husband, who claimed he was getting back together with his wife, found out she was carrying the boyfriend's baby, how would he react? Would that send him into a rage so bad that he'd strangle her?

That seemed probable. Turning it around, how would Kapur react to finding out the woman he was living with was screwing her ex-husband?

He wouldn't be happy, but it didn't seem he had as much invested in her as the ex-husband did.

***

Derrick stormed into the office. His shirt had dark circles under both arms.

"Looks like the pool guy was right; there was someone out back."

"Neighbor verified it?"

"Two houses down, a woman named Joan Carter. She said that she was in her yard, watching her dog do his business, when she saw a man walking quickly into the preserve area. Description fit what the pool tech told us."

"Same time?"

"Yep. Said her dog goes the same time every morning."

"Any of the neighbors have any cameras pointing to the rear?"

"There were two, but they're focused on their lanais."

"All right, I didn't think this was a burglary gone wrong, but we have two witnesses that saw somebody. We're going to have to talk to the people at Manor Care Health. See if anyone saw this mystery man around that time."

"That may help. But why that house?"

"You mean, if it was a robbery, why choose her house?"

"Yeah, it's not like she had a fancy house or something to target. Was it completely random?"

"It could be another person in her life, another relationship. Who knows, maybe the ex-husband hired someone to do it, and he came afterward."

"You think so?"

"Anything is possible. We're dealing with the human element. People have been creating all kinds of crazy schemes to throw law enforcement off."

"You want me to start interviewing?"

"No, get McQuire to send a couple of uniformed officers out there. I'd like you to draft a subpoena to get at George Evans' cell phone records. Keep it tight. At this point, only ask for calls between eight a.m. and ten."

"That's it?"

"We have a much stronger chance of getting it. In fact, I'd say it's guaranteed. Let's see what comes back. We can always widen it."

Chapter 8

I turned off Old 41 onto Industrial Way and pulled up to Gonzalez Green Care. Three garage doors were up, and a handful of sweat-drenched men were washing at a trough sink.

A dark-skinned man in a straw hat and long sleeves started my way. Criminals and immigrants could always pick out a cop.

"Rigoberto Gomez?"

His accent wasn't as heavy as I expected. "Yes, sir."

The red bandanna around his neck was worn Lone Ranger style. These men had to protect themselves from more than the sun.

"Thank you for coming forward. We appreciate it."

"We were real sorry to hear about the lady. She was nice."

"I'd like you to tell me what you saw the morning of March fifth, when you were at the Evans home."

"Well, we go there Tuesdays, and I was trimming the plants inside the cage. I wasn't trying to see inside the house or anything like that, but I saw the lady and a man."

"And what time was this?"

"A little before nine thirty, something like that."

"Are you certain about the time?"

"I think so. We got to the block around eight thirty, and their house is the third one."

"Okay, you saw a woman and a man. Did you recognize the woman?"

"It was the lady who owned the house."

"And the man?"

"I don't know."

"What were they doing?"

"It looked like they were arguing."

"What was the lady, Jill Evans, wearing?"

"I don't know."

"How about the man?"

"I don't know."

I took out a sketch of the house and yard. "Where were you when you saw them?"

He pointed to the left-hand corner. "I think over here."

"What plant were you trimming?"

"I don't know."

"Mr. Gomez, who are you protecting?"

"Nobody, I swear."

"Lying to an officer of the court is a crime, Mr. Gomez. Now, you didn't see anything, did you?"

He shrugged.

"Who saw them?"

"He wants to do the right thing. He's a good man. He didn't have to say anything."

"Is he illegal?"

He nodded.

"He has nothing to worry about. I don't care if he's from Mars. I'm a homicide detective, and all I'm interested in is solving this terrible murder. In fact, you never know, providing information to an investigation would look good if he applies for citizenship."

"You can help with that?"

"I can put in a good word."

"I don't know. I can't say anything. I promised."

"Look, I'll get your boss to have everyone sit down with me. He won't be happy about that, and you'd be wasting my time as well."

"Can I talk to him?"

"He's here?"

He nodded.

"Tell him he has my word; nothing is going to happen to him."

Gomez hustled around a trailer loaded with plant debris and into the building. I pulled out my phone. There was a text from Derrick asking me to call him.

"You get anywhere with the landscapers?"

"It's a long story. What's going on?"

"Just received a call from a Debra Ringer. She was a good friend of Jill Evans. We need to talk to her. She said that Evans was in a custody battle with her first husband to get her kid to live with her."

Gomez was escorting a short man in baggy khakis toward me. "Set something up for the morning with her. I got to go."

"Detective, this is Juan Espeza."

The man was looking at his boots.

"Mr. Espeza, do you speak English?"

He nodded. "Yes."

He was missing three of his top teeth. "You have nothing to worry about with immigration. I just want to know what you saw that morning. Okay?"

Espeza nodded.

"You were at the Evans house, the place where the woman was murdered, the morning it happened. Is that correct?"

"Yes, sir."

His accent was heavy.

"Where were you?"

"In the back, by the pool, cutting the palms."

"What did you see?"

"I see the lady inside and a man. They were fighting."

"You saw this through the sliding doors?"

"Yes."

"Why do you believe they were fighting?"

"I don't know. They were moving the arms, and he was following after her."

"Are you sure the woman was Jill Evans, the owner of the house?"

"Yes, she is good lady; she give me water."

"And the man; who was the man?"

"I don't know. I no see his face."

"Was he tall? Short?"

"No, normal size."

"Did he appear muscular?"

"No."

"Was he wearing glasses, or anything else you can tell me?"

"No glasses, I don't think."

"Did you hear them yelling or fighting?"

"No, no. The mowers, you no hear."

I pulled out a photo of George Evans, but he couldn't say he was the one he saw. After another fifteen minutes of questions, I thanked him, saying I may need to speak with him again.

***

I hopped into the Cherokee, and after getting a half a mile away from the landscape company, hit the lights and siren. There was a small window of time that I needed to bull's-eye.

I walked into the orange-brown building and found the manager. He asked me to wait by a couple of chairs near a fake fireplace. Did funeral directors get taught to speak in a hushed tone?

A minute later, he came out of a room with a woman and pointed in my direction. Tina Runo was dressed in black and looked to be about seventy. Her gray hair was pulled back in a bun, and her eyes were clear.

"Ma'am, I'm really sorry to have to come here today. I know how tough this is, but it couldn't wait."

"Do you have information on who did this to Jillian?"

"No, but we have an important development. Please sit. It'll only take a minute to explain."

She pursed her lips and sat.

"During the examination of your daughter's body, the coroner took blood samples. It's customary to look for any foreign substances or poisons."

She stiffened. "What did you find?"

"That your daughter was pregnant. Did you know that?"

"She was pregnant? By that Jafar person?"

"That's what we are trying to determine."

She wagged her head. "I didn't know she was with child. It's very sad. Whoever did this, killed her baby as well."

"We're going to find out and punish the person who did this. I need your help, though, in understanding who the father was."

"What can I do?"

"You're the next of kin, and we'd like your permission to take a sample of the fetus' tissue and run DNA tests on it."

"You had your opportunity, Detective. I'm not going to allow anymore poking around to be done to my Jillian. Let her rest in peace, for God's sake."

"I understand your position, ma'am, but it'll be just a needle, biopsy like. We need a small sample; that's it."

She stood up. "I'm sorry, Detective, but I can't allow that. Now, please excuse me. I have my daughter's funeral to attend."

Chapter 9

George Evans kept tugging at his blue golf shirt. He looked lipless. His pasty complexion and thin lips were the same blah color. His jittery state was evidence that my idea to question him in my office rather than in an interview room hadn't worked.

He eyed the digital recorder I put on my desk and said, "You're recording this?"

"Yes, it's standard procedure."

"What, am I a suspect?"

"It's for everybody's protection. They'll be a record of our conversation, so no one can make any assertions about who said what."

"Maybe I should get a lawyer."

"That's your right. It you want an attorney, you can ask for one. If you are unable to afford one, the county will appoint a public defender to represent you."

"I didn't do anything wrong. That I know of."

I hit record. "What do you mean by that?"

"Nothing, just that if there's some law on the books about calling nine one one or something I should have done when someone loses consciousness."

"I'd like to ask you about the nine-one-one calls."

"I told you everything that day, at the house."

"Do me a favor; let's go over it again. It's something that we do in every case. Just tell me what happened."

"I got to the house around ten in the morning, but Jill didn't answer the door. I thought something was wrong or that she was on the lanai, so I went to the back. I saw a slider was open, so I stuck my head in and called her name."

"You were divorced from her. What were you doing at her house that morning?"

"We were getting back together. Things were going good. She said that she had something to tell me and asked me to come over."

"Did she tell you what she wanted to discuss?"

"No, but I figured it had to be about us. She knew I didn't like the guy she was seeing, and I hoped she was going to end it with him."

Last time he said he had no idea what she wanted. Then he said it might be bad news. I didn't want to challenge him, put him on guard. "Would that be Jafar Kapur?"

He gave a look like he'd smelled a skunk. "Yeah."

"You stuck your head in the house and called her name. Did she answer?"

"No. So, I walked in the house to see what was going on."

"Going on?"

"Why she didn't answer is what I meant."

"Okay. Then what?"

"I found her in the kitchen, on the floor. She was knocked out. I went to see if she was breathing, but she wasn't. I tried to find a pulse, but there was nothing."

"Did you check her wrist for a pulse?"

"No, her neck. Isn't that the best place?"

"Yes. What happened next?"

"I didn't know what to do. I tried to give her mouth to mouth, but it wasn't working, and then I called nine one one for help. I followed what they said to do, but nothing worked."

"Anything else?"

"No. I waited, and then the EMT came, but they couldn't do anything for her. She was gone . . ."

"I'm sorry."

"Every time something is going good for me, it doesn't last."

"Did you move her body?"

"No. Well, just to give her the mouth to mouth."

"Let's go back to when you first saw her on the floor. Did you notice anything out of place?"

"Her bag was on the floor and the wallet was out. I immediately thought she'd been robbed, and whoever did it killed her."

"When you first came in, how did you know she was dead?"

"I, I didn't. I'm just saying what I thought."

"You thought she was dead before checking her pulse or breathing?"

"I guess so."

"Do you have any medical training?"

"No, none at all."

"Okay. Let me just make sure I have this straight for the record. Your ex-wife called you, asking you to come over but didn't tell you why. She didn't answer the door, and you went around back, entering the home via an open slider. You found her unconscious on the floor of the kitchen. You attempted to revive her without success. You made a call to nine one one. You followed their instructions, again without any change in her status, before help arrived. Is that accurate?"

"Yes, that's what happened."

"Are we leaving anything out?"

"No. That's it."

I opened my Moleskine. "I believe you told us that after administering CPR you ran outside the home looking for help."

"Oh yeah, I forgot about that. But nobody was around, and I ran right back inside. It was only for a minute or so."

"Is there anything else you may have forgotten? Take your time and think about it. You were under a tremendous amount of pressure that morning."

He shook his head. "No, that's all I remember."

"Are you sure?"

It might have been sadistic, but I enjoyed seeing him squirm like a seven-year-old that had to take a leak.

"Yes. I'm positive."

"That's funny, because there were two calls made from Jillian's phone to nine one one that morning."

"Two calls? Maybe I screwed up and hung up or something and redialed. I don't remember that, but like you say, the situation was surreal. My mind was going crazy. I didn't know what to do."

He may not have known what to do, but I knew what I had to do now. We needed to find out what he did during the time between calls.

***

Tony Robertson was the supervisor George Evans employed at Keep Cool, his defunct air-conditioning company. Robertson was now working for another HVAC company that went by the name of Comfort Climate.

You couldn't drive around for five minutes without seeing a truck on its way to fix a home's air-conditioning system. Along with pool companies and landscapers, the climate created a year-round demand for their services.

I pulled onto Hickory Boulevard and a minute later spotted the Comfort Climate truck. It was in a driveway across the street from the beach in Bonita Springs. A man was on a forklift raising an outdoor compressor to a ten-foot-high platform. Standing on the small deck, two other men worked the unit off the forklift, maneuvering it in place, above any possible water.

The height the building codes insisted on struck me as overkill. If water rose that high, having a problem with your air-conditioning would be akin to running out of peanut butter.

"Tony Robertson?"

"Yes, sir. What can I do for you?"

"Detective Luca, with the Collier County Sheriff's Office. I'd like to ask you a couple of questions."

"Me?"

"Don't worry, Mr. Robertson, it's not about you. It concerns your former employer, George Evans."

"Oh. What do you want to know?"

"How long have you known George Evans?"

"We met at Estero Air about ten years ago. I was a tech, and George was the service manager back then."

"You went to work for him at Keep Cool?"

"Yeah, when he started it, I went with him, like, two weeks after he started. I was afraid he wouldn't make it, but he was able to get a couple of commercial accounts by undercutting Estero's prices."

"How would you describe him?"

"George is a good guy but strange. Like he's distracted or something."

"Was he honest?"

"Yeah, I think so. I mean, when things were going bad, he gave me a line of bullshit about it. But he had to, you know, otherwise I would have bolted sooner than I did."

"Did he have a temper?"

"Who doesn't?"

"Is that a yes?"

"He had a rough time when things went south. The market was crashing, and work was hard to come by, and he was having problems with his wife."

"Jillian?"

"Yeah. I don't know, but he told me she was pushing for things. She liked the good life, I guess, and he couldn't keep her satisfied. I felt for the guy."

"When he'd get angry, did it get physical?"

"With me? No."

"Any coworkers, customers, anybody?"

Robertson exhaled. "Look, he was under a lot pressure at the end, and this tech, Jeremy, he screwed up big time on a job we were doing for La Playa. He was flushing out the lines and never shut the valves off. There was water everywhere. I think it cost George three grand, that he didn't have, to change out some wallboard and paint everything."

"What did he do to the tech?"

"I had to break them up. George grabbed him by the throat and had him against the wall. Jeremy kicked him in the nuts to break free, and they were throwing punches till me and another guy separated them."

"George choked him?"

"I guess so."

"Any other encounters that evidenced his anger?"

"I left right after that. In fact, I always felt I pushed him over the edge because the day before that incident was when I gave him notice that I was leaving. I felt bad because he gave me a chance to supervise, and without that I'd be up in attics sweating my ass off."

"Do you see George Evans any longer?"

He shook his head. "Nah, we never hung out socially. When I heard what happened to his wife, I wanted to call him but . . . I should have, it was the right thing to do, but I didn't know if he was still pissed at me."

"Do you think he could have been involved with the death of his wife?"

"No. He was kind of dark, you know, but not a killer."

"Even if he snapped?"

"I guess so."

Robertson provided evidence Evans had choked someone who worked for him. Not a stranger, but a person he knew, someone he gave a paycheck to. It was proof he could go off the rails. However, countering that was the stress he was under, with a business about to fold, and his wife about to leave.

Chapter 10

If it wasn't caffeine causing Debra Ringer to speak rapidly while moving her hands. I'd have to view what she said through a nervous person's prism. She was petite, platinum blond, with neon-pink lips that matched her nails.

"Okay, slow down a moment, and tell me what Jill told you."

"Well, we were good friends, you know, all the way back to junior high, and we shared everything, well, almost everything. I knew before anybody that she was leaving George."

I wasn't sure whether I should steer her back to husband number one or not. "Sounds like you've been best friends for a long time."

"Oh yeah, like I said, since before high school. We took driver's ed together. We both liked the instructor. He was handsome, just like you, Detective. We both flirted with him, you know, like a little competition to see if we could rile him up." She laughed.

Having dealt with the aftermath of a man who'd been falsely aroused by a woman and ended up forcing himself on her wasn't funny. "Tell me about her first husband."

"I remember when she met Brian. He was good for her. I mean, he was like, stable, you know? She got a little too close, too fast, and I told her to slow down. She cooled it down at first, but then they were inseparable. They got married way too quickly. I tried to tell her, but you know how it goes when somebody thinks they're falling in love, but it's really just infatuation."

"They had a child right away?"

"Yes, she was pregnant with Joyce before they came back from their honeymoon. I was afraid for her, too many changes, too quickly. I hate to say it, but I was right."

"They had problems right away?"

"Yes, but it wasn't her fault. Jill suffered from postpartum depression. It was real ugly for a long time. I mean, she gave up on life, on herself. She didn't seem to care about the baby, and she stopped taking care of Joyce. She just couldn't get out of her funk. I tried to help her, but she pushed everybody away. It was sad, and it ended up costing her custody."

"Brian and she divorced, and she gave up custody of her daughter?"

She shook her head. "Tough to believe, but that's what happened."

Tough? Impossible. I'd heard of the condition. It had to be devastating for a mother to give up her child.

"How long ago was that?"

"Well, Joyce is about ten now, so ten years ago."

"You mentioned that she was trying to get her daughter back."

"Yeah, she told me about six months ago that she was trying to get custody of Joyce."

"She had visiting rights?"

"Yeah, but like, every other weekend was basically it. Plus, they split the holidays up."

"I imagine her ex-husband wasn't too happy about it."

"He went crazy when she served him with papers, suing him for custody. Jill said the courts favored mothers and that she was going to get Joyce back."

"Why now? Why not when she was married to George Evans?"

"Jill was fragile, even when she married George. She was never the person she was before having a baby. When she got postpartum, they gave her pills. It's only supposed to last like a year at most, but I think the drugs screwed her up. I don't think she really got off them until she started up with Jafar."

"I understand that she started dating him about two years ago."

"That sounds right."

"So why go for custody now?"

"She was coming into her own, I mean, who she was before everything. Jill started having the confidence to lead her own life, you know, and she wanted to raise Joyce. She would complain that Brian didn't understand how to raise a daughter. I know Joyce was telling her this and that about Brian, but it was all just normal kid stuff to me."

"What did Jafar Kapur think about her bringing the kid into the house?"

"It didn't matter; Jill was going to dump him."

"But I thought he helped her to get back on track."

"He did, but she realized that he wasn't for her. I mean, she was grateful that he helped her, but she was moving on and wanted to break the dependency she had on him."

"Did she tell Mr. Kapur that?"

"Not that I know. You know, the funny thing is that she said that Brian hated Jafar and that he told her that no kid of his was going to live with a, this is going to sound bad, but I'm just saying what she said."

"It's okay. Tell me."

"He called him a dot head. And you know, the funny thing is, Jafar was going to be out of the picture."

If what Debra Ringer told me was even half true, we had some credible leads to follow. The news Jafar Kapur was going to get the boot was interesting. He could have flipped out over the kid moving in, or was it Jillian telling him they were done that pushed him over the edge?

It was interesting, and maybe it was because I was a new father, but I thought the most compelling information concerned Jill Evans's first husband.

How would any parent react if their child, one they raised alone, was taken from them? I couldn't imagine not being there for Jessie every day. We needed to take a close look at Brian Wild. The thought of losing custody after ten years was a boatload of motivation.

Chapter 11

From Davis Boulevard I turned onto Collier and made a left into a community named Forest Glen. I wound my way onto Jungle Plum Drive, an interesting name for a street in the tropics of Southwest Florida.

A golf course ran along the back of the homes. Dead oak tree leaves crinkled underfoot as I made my way up the driveway. I rang the bell of the white, one-story home.

Jillian Evans must have liked skinny men. Her first husband, Brian Wild, was thin, just like the other men in her life. Brown or dark sandy hair was also a commonality. I had to think that over a minute.

In the past, including my first wife, I'd been drawn to blonds, but Mary Ann was a brunette. The women in my life had similar builds as well. I guess it wasn't unusual.

Wild had a firm grip, and he looked me in the eye when we shook hands. It was something I liked in a man. His driver's license put him at forty-one, but he appeared to be pushing fifty. Working and single parenting had taken a toll.

Scanning his face, I reminded myself not to prejudice myself; he could be a killer.

"I'm sorry for your family's loss."

"Thank you. Come in."

He forced it.

The home was about twenty-two hundred feet with new tiling that look like wood. I pegged a price tag of five hundred and fifty thousand on it. We settled in the kitchen.

"I'd like to ask you a couple of questions about your former wife."

"Outside of dropping off Joyce on weekends, we didn't interact."

"I understand she suffered from postpartum depression and that led to your divorce."

"You can call it what you like. Every doctor we went to said it would pass within a year of her giving birth. Something else was going on, but I gave up trying to figure it out. I had a baby girl to take care of."

"Did you ever remarry?"

"Who has the time to date? Between working and making sure Joyce was doing good. It's not easy being a single parent. I got to cook, shop, clean, help her with homework, drop her off here and there. It's exhausting. But I'm not complaining. I love being her father."

"You have sole custody, correct?"

"Yes."

"I understand that Jillian didn't fight you over it."

"She's lucky the judge gave her visiting rights. She didn't give two shits for her own daughter. Nobody could believe it. They thought I was making this crap up. I mean, hell, if I hadn't gone through this myself, I wouldn't believe it either."

Man, was I glad Mary Ann didn't get postpartum depression. "How did you get along with your ex-wife?"

"Like I said, we don't have much contact, unless it's about Joyce."

"How was the relationship between Jillian and your daughter?"

"Look, Joyce was abandoned by her mother. She's old enough to understand that now. Then Jill wakes up one day, and all of a sudden she thinks nothing happened? She's out of her mind."

"I understand she was trying to gain custody of your daughter."

"She could try all she damn wants. It wasn't happening."

"Jillian filed a suit in family court challenging the original custody award."

"She had some balls doing that. After all we've been through, she wants to drag Joyce through all that? The kid was all torn up. She didn't want things to change, and, of course, she's only ten and didn't want to disappoint her mother. For God's sake, she was frigging afraid she'd lose her mother again."

"It made you angry that she was trying to take your daughter away?"

"Of course it did. She wasn't around to change diapers and help her walk and talk. Now, she wants to waltz in and take her from me? How fucked up is that?"

"I understand. Just for the record, can you tell me where you were the morning of March fifth?"

"What? You think I did it?"

"Please answer the question."

"I was at work."

"What place?"

"Tamiami Ford, near Naples Airport."

"What do you do there?"

"I'm the parts manager."

"What time did you get to work?"

"I don't know exactly, around eight."

I asked a few more questions before leaving him. We needed to look into his alibi, but he seemed like a regular guy who resented his ex-wife's attempt to take his daughter away from him. It was an understandable reaction, and though it was an excellent motivator, I didn't see him as the strangler.

Who was Jillian Evans? She'd changed her name from Wild to Evans but never returned to her maiden name, Runo, when her second marriage ended. Was there a reason for that?

She was trying to make up for what she lost to postpartum depression and whatever was going on after that. I understood that. Maybe she tried approaching Wild about some kind of joint custody and he rebelled. I understood that as well.

Jill Evans was trying to get her life together when she was snuffed out. Why? Who did it? We needed a rounder picture, more color on her and the people around her.

Chapter 12

I had just plugged Brian Wild's name into Collier's Record Management System, to check on any contacts with law enforcement, when Derrick leapt out of his seat.

"Holy shit! George Evans made a call from his phone at nine fifty-two a.m."

"Really? That was just a couple of minutes after he made the first nine-one-one call."

"Yeah, just three minutes, to be exact."

"Who'd he call?"

"Marshall Woodrow. And guess what he does?"

I loved Derrick, but his guessing games got under my skin. "He skydives."

"Woodrow is a lawyer."

"How long was he on the phone for?"

"Three minutes, forty seconds."

"Enough time to get advice from an attorney on what to do after you committed a homicide."

"No doubt. Maybe Evans is smarter than we think. With attorney-client privilege, neither one of them has to tell us the nature of the call."

"That's a problem."

"You think so? We have a damn good idea what the call was about."

"We still have to grill Evans on it, but I don't want him to be on guard. We start pushing for answers, he may bring in a lawyer, and then everything will have to go through his mouthpiece. I have an idea that might work."

***

Engine running, the Cool Zone truck was parked in the shade at the end of a cul-de-sac. Was Evans a slacker? Stealing time from his boss was a minor offense, but what did it say about his character?

Leaning against the headrest, Evans had his eyes shut. I knocked on the window, and his shoulders sagged. He stepped out of the van, his gray work shirt completely darkened with sweat. He'd just finished a job and was resting.

"Sorry to surprise you like that."

"Was trying to cool off. I had to go into the attic. A palm rat chewed a dozen holes in the ductwork."

"You can get back in the vehicle if you want."

"It's okay. Do you have some news for me?"

"No. I had forgotten to grab a DNA sample from you. Forensics picked up evidence of two different DNAs on Jillian's body. They were both male, and I wanted to make sure one of them matched you, so we could concentrate on finding who the other came from."

"Oh, I didn't know that. I bet you it's Jafar's."

"We're going to get a sample of his as well. In fact, I think my partner is getting it today."

"You got to check into that guy. He's as shady as they come."

"We're aware of him and are investigating his possible involvement in the homicide."

"Good."

"Now, I must advise you that providing a DNA sample is completely voluntary. You don't have to tender one, but I'd be appreciative if you did. It would save us time confirming that one of them is yours, since you were trying to revive her."

"I don't have a problem giving it."

Reaching into my pocket for a collection kit, I said, "Excellent. It's a simple procedure."

After Evans signed the consent form, I pulled on gloves and swabbed the inside of his left cheek. Ejecting the swab into a tube, I repeated the process on the right side.

"Thanks again."

"No problem."

"You'd be surprised at how many people go to a lawyer when we ask for a sample."

"A lawyer? Why would you need one if you didn't do anything?"

"Good question. I was wondering why you called Marshall Woodrow the morning Jillian was murdered. He's a lawyer, isn't he?"

His face went so pale I could finally make out his lips.

"Uh, Mr. Woodrow was the lawyer I used for my business."

"Oh, I see. But I'm certain he handles criminal law, not business law."

"I had a lot of problems with the business. I didn't do anything wrong. It just went bad, but people, they made a lot of accusations that I'd done illegal things."

"Did anyone file a criminal complaint?"

"No, but there were threats to do so."

"Why would you need a criminal attorney if there were no charges?"

"My friends were telling me I should be ready if someone did file a charge."

He expected me to believe he was being cautious over a failed business but didn't think to get counsel when his wife was murdered, and he was the one who found her?

"That seems prudent, but you called Woodrow on the morning your wife was killed. That's a coincidence that's hard to ignore. Wouldn't you agree?"

"I know how it looks, but that has nothing to do with it."

"Calling a criminal attorney at nine fifty-two a.m., a time squarely in the middle of the period the medical examiner established as the time of death, has nothing to do with it? Explain that to me."

"You see, I, I called him on the way to Jill's house. As I was driving there, I figured I'd use the time to talk to him, you know, some multitasking."

There was no reason not to ask. "What did you talk to him about?"

"Nothing."

He was stalling. "Nothing?"

"I never spoke to him."

Maybe he didn't know about the attorney-client privacy rules. "You were on the phone for more than three minutes, and you didn't talk to Marshall Woodrow?"

"I guess so, I didn't keep track of the time, but he never picked up. I was on hold waiting for him, and when I got to Jill's, I just hung up."

If he was making it up, he was quicker than a cat on his feet. He'd be a more formidable suspect than I'd expected. But if he was good under pressure, then the choking incident couldn't be discounted.

As I exited the Forest Glen golf community, the reality hit me that whether he did or didn't talk to Marshal Woodrow was meaningless. What was important was the fact he called a criminal lawyer at the time he did.

Chapter 13

Derrick hung up the phone and stood. "Wild lied about his alibi. He wasn't at work until noon."

"Who'd you check with?"

"His boss at Tamiami Ford. A guy named Roger Brown. Said Wild told him the day before he had to go the doctor and would be late."

"Why would he change his story?"

"Because he's the one who killed Evans."

"If it was him, it was premeditated."

"He was so pissed off at her for trying to get custody of the kid that he decided killing her was the way to prevent him from losing his daughter."

"I wonder if he contacted an attorney. It could be that they told him family court judges would grant her joint custody."

"Or maybe there is something he's hiding that, if it came out, he'd lose custody."

"Could be. Jill may have known it and threatened him."

"Wild felt boxed in and lost it."

"We need to make sure the Ford dealer has the date right. Why don't you take a ride down there? There has to be some record keeping to verify it."

Derrick reached for his jacket. "On my way."

"While you're there, talk to a couple of his coworkers. See what they tell you about him, but don't make it obvious we're interested in the Evans case."

***

An email came in from the forensics lab. The DNA sample I'd collected from George Evans matched one of the two found on Jillian's body. It was no surprise. He was there that morning. The question was whether the DNA transfer occurred from trying to revive her or from strangling her.

What was somewhat interesting was the lack of his DNA on either Jillian's handbag or wallet. It didn't say much about whether he staged it or not. Anyone who watched TV knew to wear gloves or use a cloth to handle things.

We learned nothing.

***

My attempt to get permission to sample the fetus that died with Jill Evans went nowhere. Her mother was steadfast in her denial. Had I made a mistake going to Naples Memorial Gardens yesterday? On reflection, it seemed insensitive, but what was I supposed to do? The burial was less than a day away.

In order to determine who the father was, I'd have to request an exhumation. It was a delicate and uncommon process. Sheriff Chester would have to back the effort if we expected a court to grant us the authority.

I buttoned the top of my shirt as I was shown in. Chester was reading a report.

"Take a seat, Frank."

Frank? That was a good sign. I never knew if the sheriff had purposely redirected the air-conditioning vent. Both chairs in front of his desk could be used to keep fish fresh. A no-nonsense guy, Chester loathed long meetings and was a world-class manipulator.

He put the document down and took his readers off.

"How is Mary Ann and the baby?"

"All is good, sir. Thanks for asking."

"Before we get into this exhumation business, give me a rundown on where you are with the Evans case."

Chester always read the progress reports I'd submitted. Maybe it was the fact he hadn't been on the streets in a long time and liked to banter a bit.

"It's going well. We have a couple of interesting developments that center the suspect list around the men in her life. Her second husband, the one who called it in, is probably the primary, but her first husband, who has custody of their daughter, is moving up."

"What prompted that?"

"He gave us an alibi that washed out."

"Could be a mix-up in dates. Was he seen with the victim recently?"

"Doesn't seem to be much more interaction than dropping the kid off for visitation. But here's the thing, she sued to take custody from him."

"Powerful motivator."

"Exactly."

"Have you ruled out a burglary?"

"No. We're looking into a witness who saw a man in the preserve by the crime scene."

"And how is this all related to your interest in an exhumation?"

"We believe knowing who the father was will clarify motivation."

A frown was all I got.

"You see, sir, it could be that the boyfriend learned she was impregnated by her ex-husband, and it threw him into a rage. Or the ex-husband was the father. They were in the midst of a reconciliation, according to him. If it was the ex, maybe she told him she wanted to abort the baby and he lost it."

"That appears to be a stretch."

"It's an important piece of discovery. We're early in this, but knowing who the father was will save time."

"Or prejudice the investigation."

"That will not happen, sir."

"An exhumation will draw the press out like mosquitoes. Who knows what the mother will do. Maybe it's the macabre element in all of us, but everyone is fascinated when a body is dug up."

"I believe it's our desire to see what is going to happen to all of us, sir."

"Feeling philosophical?"

"It's either that or resurrection hopes."

"My concern is in drawing attention to this. You know the mother will be in the papers saying she opposed it, and public opinion will go against the department. You're a father now, you know how upsetting this will get."

"No doubt, sir, I feel for the mother and wouldn't make the request if I felt it wasn't necessary."

"And there's the cost of this. We have to be mindful of the expense. We don't have a limitless budget."

That was total bullshit. I wanted to tell him what the cost would be if word got out that Naples wasn't as safe as people thought. Chester always threw money out to deflect. He didn't want the attention an exhumation would bring.

"If the information we obtain helps to solve this case, we'll save on overtime, sir."

"Let me think this over."

That meant no. He was being political. I knew how to play this game as well. The problem was I hated doing so. In this case, I'd get what we needed by coming back if we hit a wall.

Taking the stairs down, I knew that if he didn't budge at that time, I might have to drop a leak to the press to get him to see the light.

***

Derrick looked up from his screen. "Chester said no. Didn't he?"

"Yep. As soon as he started with the budgetary bullshit, I knew it was over for now."

"He doesn't want to see it in the papers."

"Bingo."

The phone rang, and he picked it up.

"Dickson . . . uh-huh . . . how do you spell that?"

He scribbled onto a pad, said thank you, and hung up.

"We have Brian Wild's attorney. It's a guy named Gordon Heygrid."

"Never heard of him, but he's a family-law attorney."

"You want to go see him?"

"He's not going to give us much of anything for sure. Let me try talking to him over the phone. Give me the number."

"Mr. Heygrid?"

"Yes. Who's calling?"

"Homicide Detective Frank Luca, with the Collier County Sheriff's Office."

"Homicide?"

"Yes. I understand you were representing a Brian Wild in a custody case."

"That's correct. What is this about?"

"When Mr. Wild came to you about the attempt by his ex-wife to challenge the custody suit, what did you tell him?"

"Come now, Detective, you know that information is protected by attorney-client privilege."

"Yes, I'm aware that your conversations are guarded. I was hoping that you would consider being helpful given what happened to Jillian Evans."

"I'd like to help, but there really is nothing I ethically can reveal about the case."

"Who was the judge handling the case?"

"Miriam Withers."

"Oh, I remember her from my days in the domestic violence unit. She was tough on delinquent dads. I remember this case we worked, the mother was a druggie, and we responded to a call. The kids were left alone while she went out to do a buy. The woman never came back. It was the second time she did it. I was sure she was going to lose custody, but Withers cut the mother a break."

"That's not unusual, Detective. Family court judges almost always favor mothers."

Chapter 14

The name Doris Parker had come up three times, including a confirmation by Debra Ringer that Parker had been a good friend of the victim. She seemed like the perfect person to talk to.

Parker must be some hairdresser. She was operating out of a salon on a corner of Fifth Avenue that was in the heart of the action. I took the stairs trying to imagine how we were going to chat between the hair blowers and chattering.

I knocked on a door that proclaimed Parker Hair Designs and swung it open. The room had one chair, a sink for washing, and a comfortable sitting area. The smell of rosemary hung in the air.

The space surprised me. It was nice but small. A woman with tinfoil in her hair was reading a magazine.

Wearing a black smock and blue gloves, a woman smiled at me. "Welcome. I'm Dorothy. How can I help you?"

Parker had a blond pixie haircut and earrings that almost reached her shoulders.

"I called earlier. I wanted to speak with you about a friend of yours."

"Oh sure." She turned to the woman and fiddled with her hair. "Fran, you've got another fifteen minutes. I'll be right back."

We stepped into a corridor that overlooked a series of restaurants. Most of the outdoor tables were filled with diners having lunch and sipping cocktails. It always amazed me how many people went out to fancy lunches in Naples.

I showed her my badge. "I know you're busy. But before we start, I'm curious. Tell me about your setup here."

"I'm on my own. Each of us rent our spaces. That way we don't have to give up half of what we earn to an owner. It's not for everybody, but if you have the client base to do it, it's the way to go."

"Good for you."

"You have a nice head of hair. The salt and pepper reminds me of George Clooney."

"It's more salt than pepper these days."

"We can help with that. You'd be surprised at how many men I cut and dye."

"I'll keep that in mind. Let me ask you, how long did you know Jillian Evans?"

"Believe it or not, she used to be a client of mine. I cut her hair for years."

I didn't know anything about the hair business, but her workspace and location had to be expensive. That meant two-hundred-dollar cuts, something not in Jillian Evans' league.

"She came here?"

"No. We were friends. I'd cut her hair at the house."

"I understand you knew her well."

"Yeah, we really got along. I still can't believe what happened."

"What can you tell me about her?"

"Jill was a warm person but vulnerable. She'd been through a lot when she got depressed after Joyce was born. I mean it got pretty dark; she couldn't function. I think the pills they were giving her screwed her up even more. And then she had this terrible guilt about losing her daughter. She was a mess."

"I understand she started to rebound recently."

"When Jill met George, she was doing better. He seemed to help her. I think she was thinking that if she had a baby with him it would help her forget about what had happened with Joyce."

"They didn't have any kids, right?"

"No. She did an about-face after he struck her."

"George Evans hit Jillian?"

"Sad to say, but that's what happened."

"How long ago was this?"

"I think it was about a year before she left him."

"Were there any other instances of physical abuse?"

"Not that she told me, but I advised her to leave him right then and there, but she wouldn't. So, it may have happened again, and she just may have never said anything to me."

"What do you know about George Evans?"

"Other than giving Jill some stability, and I'm not discounting it, she needed it, there was something about him that, was like, distant. You know what I mean?"

No, I have no idea what you meant. "Could you elaborate on that?"

"It's just that he was there, but he wasn't. You know? He was quiet, dark, and he was married before, like Jill was."

"I understand that she was doing well since meeting Jafar Kapur."

She rolled her eyes. "You ask me, it had nothing to do with that creep. Jill was finally realizing she was a good person and that what had happened with Joyce wasn't her fault. She learned to accept what had happened and was moving on."

This lady didn't like Jafar either. Were there any men she approved of, or was her friend just a poor judge of character?

"What bothered you about Jafar?"

"He was full of himself. An arrogant bullshit artist is what he is. He talks like he's going to save the world, but I think he's a phony. And he's a frigging control freak."

"Was he controlling with Jill?"

"Oh, definitely, and jealous as well."

"George said that he and Jill were getting back together. Is that true?"

"Yes. I thought it was stupid and told her so."

"How did Jafar deal with that?"

"Not well. He went berserk when he found out."

"What happened?"

"She just said he flipped out, and they had a massive argument."

"We were told that she was or had lost interest in both men."

"That's true. She finally felt strong enough to go out on her own."

"Are there any other people, male or female, in Jill's life that I should know about? Anyone that could have possibly done this to her?"

"Well, there was no love lost between her first husband and her. But that was a crazy situation." She looked at her watch. "There was this one guy, Barry Eisner. I didn't know the guy other than what Jill told me about him."

"What did she say?"

"Just that he was really good-looking, kinda like you." She smiled. "But she said she was done with him because he'd been arrested, not once but twice, and she had to bail him out."

"Do you know what he was charged with?"

"Pretty sure it was assault."

"Was this a recent relationship?"

"Yeah. It was pretty new. I don't know how she juggled him with George and Jafar. But he's somebody you should check out."

"I'll look into that. Is there anything else you can tell me?"

"Jill wasn't a threatening person. She was a lost soul finding herself. I guess some people took that for weakness."

Chapter 15

I was almost home, just ten minutes away from seeing Jessie, when a call came over the radio. Dispatch was broadcasting a request to respond to a domestic violence report. The address, in the opposite direction, was five minutes away.

I glanced at the handset, pausing before grabbing it and responding that I was in transit. The operator confirmed the name of the caller as Jenny Robbins and that it was the first time an incident had been called in from the address.

Putting the lights and siren on, I turned onto Pine Ridge and headed toward Livingston Road.

Making a right into Livingston Lakes, I drove around Palmer Lake Circle, stopping in front of a building housing four coach homes. Throwing the door open, I jogged up the driveway. A woman standing outside of a second-story home pointed to the first-floor unit.

I rang the bell, but who could hear it over the man yelling inside the apartment? I began pounding the door and was about to shoulder it open when it swung wide open.

I stuck my badge in the man's sweaty, red face. "What do you want?"

The smell of beer hit me. "Step outside."

"You can't tell me what to do."

I heard a woman crying. "Step outside the house, or I'll cuff your ass and throw you in the back of the car."

Glassy-eyed, he was about thirty pounds heavier than me. Scowling, he looked me up and down and stepped toward me. I moved aside as a marked car pulled up.

"What's your name?"

"Jake Robbins."

"Who's inside?"

"My wife."

"Stay right here. You move, and I'll arrest you. You hear me?"

He shrugged.

I shouted to the officer walking up the drive. "Keep your eye on him."

Stepping into the house, I said, "Ma'am, I'm with the police. Are you okay?"

The apartment had an open floor plan. A kitchen chair had been knocked over, and a pair of slippers were twenty feet apart. A soccer game was on the TV, and a table by a recliner was loaded with beer bottles.

The sobbing came from the closed door just off the main room. I knocked softly on it.

"Mrs. Robbins. I'm Detective Frank Luca with the sheriff's office. Can you open the door please?"

The door cracked open. A skinny woman with dark hair and a ripped shirt stared at her feet. My stomach lurched when I saw the bruise on her right cheek.

"Are you okay, ma'am?"

Sniffling, she nodded.

"You want to tell me what happened?"

"Nothing."

"You called nine one one and have a fresh bruise on your face. What happened?"

"We had a little fight, that's all."

"Over what?"

"It's private."

"If you don't tell me, I'll have no choice but to take the both of you to the station."

"No, that's not necessary."

"Good, now tell me."

She looked at her bare feet and said, "Jake had too much to drink, and he wanted to, you know, have sex, but I wasn't feeling well and told him no. He kept bothering me and trying to, you know, get me interested, but I told him to stop and he got mad."

"So, he hit you?"

She nodded.

My hand went to the butt of my gun. I took a deep breath. "He assaulted you because you weren't feeling good enough to have sex? Is that right?"

She nodded.

"Did he strike you anywhere else besides your face?"

"No."

"Would you like medical attention?"

She shook her head.

"I assume you'll file a complaint against him."

"No, I can't do that."

"Yes, you can, and you should."

"No, let's just forget it happened. I'm okay, really I am."

"We're going to arrest your husband."

"No, no. It'll make it worse. He's going to get really mad."

I'd made one mistake letting a wife talk me out of arresting a husband who'd hit her, and I wasn't going to make that error again.

"It won't be a formal arrest. We'll bring him in, make sure he's calmed down sufficiently and warn him to keep his damn hands off you."

"But—"

"Sorry, ma'am, I have to do my job."

The fact was, if she didn't press charges, we were limited in what we could do. She started crying, but I knew I had to scare this bastard, otherwise he'd be pulling the same shit before the week was over.

I told the officer to call for an EMT to take a look at her bruise and to sit with her until I came back.

The husband said, "She don't need no medical care. It was just a little argument."

"Come with me."

"Where?"

"I said come with me."

"You got to tell me where you're going."

"I don't have to tell you anything. If you want, I can cuff your ass. Now, get in the back seat."

He climbed in, and I drove down the street.

"Where you going?"

"You like to hit women? You're a coward, that's what you are."

"It was an accident."

"An accident? That's what you're calling it now? You have any sisters?"

He shook his head.

"Figures. Your father beat your mother? Is that how you became an animal?"

"I ain't no animal."

I pulled over a mile from his house. "You damn sure are. How would you like it if you had a daughter, and she was being abused physically by a man? How'd that make you feel?"

"Aw, come on, man."

I resisted the urge to smack the butt of my gun into the side of his face. "I asked you, how would it make you feel?"

"You know it would piss me off."

"So, why the hell did you hit her? She's someone's daughter. I'm telling you, if you so much as raise a hand to her, I'll get you, and you'll pay for it. You hear me?"

He nodded.

"You'd better not touch her. I'm keeping an eye on you. If you do, you'll regret it. Trust me. Now get out."

"Here?"

"Damn right. You're walking back."

As he got out, fat raindrops began to pelt the windshield. It felt like God was partnering with me.

Chapter 16

For some reason I could not explain, I had a bad feeling as I headed to work. Was it because I was up half the night worrying that Jessie would get into some hellish relationship with a bully? Or was something else just below the surface about to rear its ugly head?

Trying to sort out the source of the anxiety as I drove to work, my cell rang. It was Sheriff Chester. He wanted to see me immediately. It looked like I was about to find out what was making me nervous.

Chester was wearing a yellow tie and a grim look. There was a smell I couldn't identify in the air.

"Sit down, Frank."

"What did you want to see me about, sir?"

"Were you informed about the robbery two nights ago at Cote d'Azur?"

It was Indian food the sheriff was a fan of that smelled. "Yes. I understand an older couple was robbed at their vehicle."

"Correct. They had just eaten and were getting into their car. Two masked men approached them. They drew guns and took their money, jewelry, and cell phones. The husband was in his eighties and almost had a heart attack. They had to bring him to NCH."

"Disgusting, sir. But it could just have been a couple of kids or junkies."

"I don't think so. Last night the patrons of the Capital Grille were robbed."

"What? Inside the restaurant?"

"I am afraid so."

"How come I didn't hear anything about it?"

"We asked them to keep it quiet as long as possible. But it's only a matter of time. I'd say tonight's evening news will be filled with stories on it."

"What happened?"

"A team of eight, they had masks on but were probably all male, entered the restaurant. They grabbed the hostess and split into groups of two. Guns drawn, they went into each of the rooms. The robbers forced all diners to lie on the floor and took their wallets, phones, and jewelry. One of them ripped out the house phone, and the gang was out in under five minutes. They hopped into a dark blue van and proceeded north on Forty-One. The van was found in the parking lot of Arthrex on Immokalee. It was stolen."

"What do they think this is, Baltimore? I can't believe I'm hearing this."

"Neither can I. As you know, this is deeply concerning."

"You mentioned the Cote d'Azur robbery earlier. What did that have to do with the Capital Grille crime?"

"They're related."

"I don't understand. They seem totally different."

"The perpetrators in both robberies were wearing Popeye masks."

At least the thieves had a sense of humor. "Are we certain, sir? These are two very different types of crimes."

"I agree, but that's the report I was given. It's the reason I want you to handle the investigation."

"Me? But sir, I'm in the middle of the Evans homicide case, and Detective Roberts and his squad are more than capable—"

"Roberts took leave yesterday. His father is very ill, and he's gone to Michigan to be with him."

"I'm sorry to hear that, but he has a good team—"

Chester leaned in. "We have to apprehend these thugs immediately. If they strike again, the damage it will do to tourism will be in the hundreds of millions."

The sheriff was right on that count. If there was a band of armed thieves robbing and terrorizing diners, no one, locals included, would go out to eat in Naples. I didn't want to put the Evans case aside, but this case had larger implications if it wasn't solved.

***

My chest-high pile of things to work on had just been given steroids by Chester, but I had two visits that I'd promised myself I'd make. Pelican Larry's was a bar that had food. The cigarette smoke from the outdoor bar made me hold my breath as I searched for her. When Jenny Robbins saw me, she nearly dropped the tray of food she was carrying.

I waved. "Hiya doing? Can I have five minutes?" I pointed to the indoor bar and took a stool wondering if she thought I was here to hit on her.

Wiping her hands on her apron, Jenny approached me. "Can I get something for you?"

"No thanks. I just stopped in to make sure you're okay."

She looked both ways. "Everything is fine."

"Good. It better stay that way. Look, I don't want you to get the wrong impression about me. I have a little girl, and I'm concerned about any woman living with an abusive husband and I—"

"Jake's not abusive."

I lowered my voice. "Just listen to me, okay? You don't have to put up with that bullshit. He lays a hand on you, you get the hell out of there as fast as possible. You can call the cops a hundred times, but if you're not going to realize you have to leave him, nothing is going to change. You understand?"

She nodded.

"Okay, call us if you need us."

I couldn't understand why so many women stayed with abusive men. It made me so damn angry that they didn't realize how much better off they'd be if they broke the hold these cowardly men had over them. I slammed the Cherokee door shut and pulled out of the parking lot.

It took me fifteen minutes to make my way to Headpinz Entertainment. The complex on Radio Road had updated bowling for the younger generation. With all the lights and music, the place should have been sitting on the Vegas Strip. I saw him as soon as I entered. He was behind the counter talking to a coworker.

I caught his eye and strolled to the other side of the place. Every time I looked over my shoulder, he was staring at me. I watched a couple bowl a few frames and walked back to the other end, passing him again. Jake Robbins was alone. I turned around and went up to the counter.

"Can I help you?"

"Nice place. It's my first time."

"You should bowl a game."

"You should keep your hands to yourself."

His Adam's apple bobbed.

"Bad things happen to men who hit women. You better be careful."

"Is that a threat?"

"Nope, a statement."

"If you're not going to use the facilities, then I'll have to ask you to leave."

"I'm going anyway, but I wanted to make sure you knew that I'm keeping my eye on you. You understand?"

It was childish, but it felt good putting a scare in him. The feeling lasted under a minute as the reality that my daughter could fall into such a treacherous relationship occupied my mind. Society needed to find a solution to tamp down aggressive behavior toward women, but I wasn't going to wait for that. I was going to do whatever I could to keep all women, and especially my kid, safe.

Chapter 17

Jessie was in her swing in front of the TV. A cartoon was playing, but she was more interested in rubbing her favorite teddy bear's nose than watching a bunch of balloon characters.

We had to be mindful of how much TV she watched. It was a cheap babysitter, but who knew the long-term ramifications of the garbage that was on 90 percent of the time? I'd fight like crazy to keep her from being brainwashed by Hollywood and the army of marketeers that ran things.

"Hi, Jessie, Daddy's home."

I slipped her out of the swing. Jessie gave me a huge smile as I held her overhead.

"She loves when you do that."

I caught a whiff of something nasty. "I know. I think she needs to be changed."

"Give her to me; I'll take care of it. You get changed."

I followed her to the changing table. "You're not going to believe this, but Chester put me on a burglary—"

"The Capital Grille robbery?"

"How'd you know about it?"

She took off Jessie's diaper, and I stepped back. "It's been on the news all day. That's some brazen way to rob."

"Chester is concerned how it will affect tourism."

"He's right. I couldn't believe it myself. If this happens again, I'd think twice about going out, especially with Jessica."

"Don't worry, little lady, Captain Marvel to the rescue."

She cleaned Jessie up and took a fresh diaper out. "Just be careful, Frank. This gang sounds dangerous."

For the first time in too long there was no tension between us. The opening I was looking for to talk the Jimena issue over with Mary Ann was there. "Don't worry. Between me and Derrick, we'll handle it. Derrick has a lot of experience with gangs up in DC."

"Good. Go get changed. I made pasta and mushrooms for you."

Pasta ai funghi? Was that a sign the undeclared war was over? I headed to the bedroom and slowly undressed. What should I do? Her going around me wasn't something I could let slide. Was it?

It was about our marriage, our partnership. We didn't do things alone anymore; we were a couple. I pulled on shorts, thinking if the opportunity arose, I was going to say something, and went into the kitchen.

"You feel like some wine?"

"It's up to you."

I headed to the closet to grab a bottle. "I want to try an Oregon Pinot Noir. I was reading they're like French Burgundy in style. Not big and fruity like the ones from California. I'm betting it goes together with the mushrooms, like God made the pairing."

"Better than the two of us?"

Did she run up a big shopping bill at Waterside today?

***

I picked up the coffee Derrick always brought me and took a sip without checking if it had too much milk. The kid was a quick learner.

"Thanks, as usual, partner."

"My pleasure. You have a good night?"

Actually, it was an amazing night, but I don't share that type of stuff. "It was a good one."

"You square things away with Mary Ann?"

He knew? "What are you talking about?"

"The whole thing with the babysitter. You were pretty upset about it."

"It's all good now." Even though Mary Ann and I never discussed it.

"Good, you have to let some things go. We all make mistakes, and whatever she did was for the good of Jessica."

I'd have to think about reframing it in that light.

"What, you? Make mistakes?"

"How much time you got?"

"We need to get moving on this restaurant gang. Chester has increased patrols in Mercato, Fifth Avenue, and Third Avenue South."

"I know they hit Mercato, but I don't see these guys going to a place they know we're going to be watching."

"I told Chester the same thing. We have restaurants all over the place. I wish it was concentrated, but it's not. He said he was going to get some major overtime approved and would up the marked-car presence around town."

"Good. We'll get them."

"We don't have much of an organized crime scene down here. The pocketbook crew that was hitting Waterside was small fish compared to these guys. I have to hand it to them; this gang has balls."

"You know, we dealt with this mind-set up in DC. They didn't do upscale restaurants because all the politicians had protection, but the mentality of the mob approach is the same: storm a place with a bunch of people, grab the loot, and run."

"They're in and out before people realize what is going on."

"It's the shock effect. We had some people with carry permits in DC who couldn't react."

"That's bullshit. They weren't trained properly. They should have their damn permits pulled before they get themselves killed."

"You're right. Man, I wish somebody would pull a gun on one of these guys."

"No. It'd be a disaster. There's no telling how far things could escalate. Remember, there are at least eight, plus a driver, that we know of. They could have a diner or two planted in the restaurant signaling them."

"I never thought about that. You think it's possible?"

"Sure, it is. What we need to understand is just how sophisticated these people are. If they're higher than they appear, they very well could have spotters and plants."

"I understand, but I don't think they're too polished. The episode with that couple doesn't fit. Way too risky."

He was right. "I've been trying to figure what the hell that was about. Maybe they were casing the restaurant, and they seemed like an easy mark. But that would show a lack of discipline."

"To me, it feels like we're dealing with a mob mentality. Rush in with a force, scare the hell out of everybody, grab and run. We had many of those types of incidents at jewelry stores and the like in DC."

Sometimes I gave criminals too much credit in the intelligence column. "Let's proceed as if they're not too sophisticated. It'll be easier to nail them if they're not. What I want to do is get some information, any detail we can on these guys. Then we'll circulate the word with our informers, and see what turns up."

"I have the financial crimes unit checking for activity on any of the diners' credit cards."

"If they used any of them, it would have been in the hour or two after the robbery."

Chapter 18

It was clear to me that the kids parking cars might be able to provide something that a terrorized diner couldn't. Five Star Valet operated all of the valet services in Mercato.

Twenty-three-year-old Robbie Daniels was working the night of the Capital Grille robbery. He was studying for his master's degree and paying for school with the big tips he collected. Five bucks was the minimum for valeting your vehicle these days and the reason I always self-parked.

I waited until the stream of expensive vehicles carrying people out for lunch slowed. Daniels was jogging back to the station after parking a Maserati when I approached and introduced myself.

"You were working the night of the robbery."

"Yeah, I didn't know what was going on until I saw them running out to over there." He pointed to an access road behind the restaurant that led to Route 41.

"Tell me what you saw."

"I was texting back and forth with my girlfriend. It was quiet out here; everyone was eating."

"What time was that?"

"About a quarter to eight."

"Go on."

"Out of the corner of my eye, I saw some guys walking behind me into the restaurant."

I was hopeful an outdoor diner might have seen something. "From the patio side?"

"No, the other side."

"Were they wearing masks?"

"I don't know. I was facing the parking lot. It just looked like a bunch of men. I figured they were a group of golfers or something."

"Did you hear them talking?"

"It's too far to hear anything, with the cars on Forty-One."

"When they exited the restaurant, where were you?"

"I didn't move. It was only about five minutes, but I heard someone say, 'Move it,' and I turned around. There were a bunch of guys running toward a dark colored van. They jumped in and took off. I saw them turn onto Forty-One. They went up, toward Bonita."

"Was a driver waiting in the vehicle for them?"

"I couldn't tell."

"Did you notice anything about the men?"

"What do you mean?"

"Anything—hair, body size, a limp, or the way they moved."

"You know, one of them definitely had something like a limp, the way he was running was like he'd had a stroke or something. You know that movie, *The Usual Suspects*, like the guy who faked his limp."

"Left side or right?"

Daniels closed his eyes for a moment. "Right side, for sure."

"What about any of their sizes? Anyone tall, short, heavy?"

"Pretty much medium, but one guy, the last one, he had a belly, not obese or anything, just when he was getting in the van I saw his gut from the side."

"What about their heights?"

"Nothing stood out."

"What were they wearing?"

"All of them were in dark clothing. Two of them with long sleeves. I remember that because it was hot."

"The heavy guy, the limper?"

"You know what? One of them was the guy with a limp. He had a black long-sleeved shirt on."

I gave him my card, telling him to think some more about it and call with anything that came to mind.

***

Dave and Mildred McGregor lived in Kensington, a North Naples community on Airport Pulling Road. I loved its location, between Vanderbilt Beach and Immokalee Road.

It was another well-kept community featuring a mix of condos and homes in a range of prices. The McGregors lived on Alberton Court in the first floor of a coach home. The flooring was all white tile, dating the home to around twenty-five years old.

Dave McGregor had snow-white hair and a matching mustache. He extended a liver-spotted hand and welcomed me into their house.

"Nice to meet you, Detective."

"Likewise."

"Mildred, the police officer is here."

A bird of a woman in tennis whites bounded out of the kitchen and smiled. "Hi, I'm Mildred McGregor."

"Thanks for taking the time to speak with me."

"Oh, you're not bothering us. After tennis, we don't do much until dinnertime."

She waved me into the kitchen, which they had half updated with new countertops. We sat down, and I handed them my card.

"Homicide? Oh my God, David, we could have been killed."

"Don't get nervous, ma'am. There is no evidence the men who robbed you were anything more than thieves. The sheriff wants this case solved quickly and asked that I assist on it."

Dave said, "I saw the news about the Capital Grille robbery. It's the same gang, isn't it?"

"We believe what happened to you may be related. What I need to know is what you remember about the men who accosted you in the parking lot."

Dave said, "We'd just come out of Cote d'Azur after dinner and went to our car. We were parked in the aisle where all those rental cars are."

Mildred said, "Avis has a store there."

I knew the restaurant. It was a favorite with the older set. The food was good, but the decor dated back to the sixties. And I'd heard it was super expensive.

"Go on."

"I was opening the door for Mildred when I heard someone say, 'Hold it right there. Don't move, and nobody will get hurt.' I don't hear so good, so I turned around, and there were these two men with Popeye masks on."

"We thought it was a joke. One of the waiters was always joking with us, and we thought it was him, right Dave?"

"Until I saw the gun, then I became alarmed." He lowered his voice. "It was frightening. I was worried over our safety."

Mildred grabbed his hand. "You never know what these drug addicts will do."

"Was there something they did that makes you believe they were drug addicts?"

Mildred said, "Who else would do something like that?"

She should only know what goes on in my world. "At this time, we don't know, but we'll apprehend the individuals responsible. Now, is there anything you can tell me about the suspects? How they looked? What they may have said?"

"We couldn't see what they looked like. They had masks on."

"I realize that. But what about their body types? Heavy, tall, maybe short?"

The couple looked at each other for a moment, and Dave said, "They were regular-sized men. If it weren't for the gun, I would have fought to keep our things."

"It's never a good idea, even if they are unarmed. You can't tell how encounters like this could turn out. You did the right thing."

"We can replace what they took."

"Not my father's watch. That's gone forever. It was a one-of-a-kind Patek Philippe. It was a Calatrava model from 1932."

There was almost no chance he'd get it back, but I said, "You never know, Mr. McGregor; there's a chance we'll be able to locate it. I'm sure it had a serial number. Do you have that somewhere?"

"Yes. The paperwork is in our lockbox."

"When you have an opportunity, get the serial number to me."

"Absolutely. I hope you can recover it. I was hoping to pass it on to my grandson, Trevor."

Mildred said, "We'll get him something, don't worry. He probably doesn't want an old man's watch anyway."

"It's not an old man's watch; it's a family heirloom."

"Getting back to the thieves, anything else you can tell me?"

"Well, one of them had an accent. I'm sure it was Spanish, and he had a limp."

"What side was he dragging?"

"His right side."

"And this man, he had an accent you believe was Spanish?"

"Yes, not heavy, but it was noticeable."

We had something to go on. It was the same crew that did both jobs. They were professionals using masks and gloves. One of its members had a limp and spoke with what was believed to be a Spanish accent.

Chapter 19

Freezing the frame, I stared at the image of a man at the pharmacy counter. He'd used a Visa credit card belonging to one of the Capital Grille diners. This was a welcome but confusing blunder.

The time line told a story that after dumping the van on Immokalee, they jumped onto Interstate 75, getting off at the next exit. They proceeded west on Bonita Springs Road to the CVS on the corner of Imperial Parkway.

The black-clad man in the video handed the pharmacist a prescription in the name of the credit card holder. It was a complete forgery, using a prescription pad that was stolen from a doctor's office. He was likely a part of the gang, but he didn't limp.

What was interesting was that H.P. Acthar was the drug bought. It was an anti-inflammatory used by multiple sclerosis patients and gout sufferers who couldn't handle the side effects of steroids.

What was even more interesting was the cost of the injectable gel medicine. It was four thousand dollars a dose.

Were we dealing with a group with a member who was sick? Or was it a family member? Were the brazen robberies an attempt to find a way to pay for a life-changing drug?

I checked into the possibility it was used to treat the gout. It was a painful condition that affected the joints, where sharp crystals usually settled in the big toe. It would slow someone down, but it didn't appear that a sufferer would have a limp.

It was beginning to feel like the limping man had MS. Partly looking for clues and partly out of curiosity, I researched the disease.

The degenerative condition that eroded the nerves' protective coating was sobering.

Most people afflicted with MS had trouble walking, which dovetailed with one of the suspects. Presently, no cure existed, only drugs that treated symptoms of the three hundred thousand Americans with the disease.

Math wasn't my strong suit, but this was pretty simple. There were roughly three hundred million people in the States. That meant about one tenth of a percent of us had MS. Florida had over twenty-one million residents. That would equate to approximately twenty thousand MS patients. Way too large a number to sort through.

Taking it to the county level, we had about a million people living in Lee and Collier, equating to about a thousand individuals. We could check with doctors and clinics in Lee and Collier Counties that specialized in dealing with MS, narrowing it down by gender and age, if we could get past privacy concerns.

If I didn't have to deal with all the legal nonsense and barriers, I could take off two days a week and still have the same solve rate.

***

Chester wanted to see me. I knew it was coming. The press was doing their best to scare everyone. Watching the news last night, I couldn't believe the coverage. Countless tourists were being interviewed on Fifth Avenue about whether they were worried they'd get caught up in another robbery.

Many vacationers seemed to brush off the threat. Was that because where they came from they had higher crimes rates? Or was it because they were here for a good time? Notably, almost a third of them expressed concern and said they were altering their dining plans.

As I trudged up the stairs, I wondered whether the networks orchestrated the mix of people the same way they manipulated other news stories.

It had been a long day, and the sheriff's green tie was loosened and his sleeves rolled up. A couple of newspapers sat on the corner of his desk.

"Take a seat, Frank."

"Thank you, sir."

"I read your report on the Popeye incidents, and I need you to step it up. Considerably."

He knew this wasn't magic. A certain amount of investigation was necessary to close any case. "We have several promising leads, and I don't want to raise expectations too high, but we're closing in."

"Expectations?" He lifted a file off his desk. "This is from the chamber of commerce. They polled their membership. Restaurant covers are down by fifteen percent. Do you know how devastating that is?"

"I understand, sir."

"If this isn't solved quickly, layoffs are going to occur, in high season. God forbid we have another event."

Event? Incidents? Chester's use of words in describing raw crime readied him for politics.

"We're working to shut these thugs down."

"Do you need anything? Manpower? Overtime authorizations?"

"I appreciate the offer, sir. At the moment, I believe we are fine. However, I'll give this more thought and come back to you if I need anything."

***

One of my favorite things to do was reading to Jessie. Tonight, I was reading *Papa, Get the Moon for Me*. Mary Ann thought it was a bit self-serving, but Jessie wouldn't know about that. Besides, she loved the book.

Jessie fell asleep in my lap in the middle of the book. I put her in her crib and stared at her. She was the picture of innocence. It was my job to protect her and the millions of kids like her.

"That was fast."

"I know. We didn't even get to the part where Papa saves the day."

"You're too much."

We stood by her crib. "She is really something. We have to do everything we can to protect her from the crap out there."

"She's going to be fine, Frank."

"Especially when she starts with the boy stuff. Jessie has to know how a man should act with a woman. None of this physical bullshit. I swear, I'd kill the guy if he laid a frigging pinky on her."

"Relax. The way we're teaching her, she'll be fine."

"I'm not as confident as you. Now that you're back on the job, you're seeing the same crap I do."

"You're focusing too much on the negative. Nobody covers the thousands of planes that land safely each day. It's the crashes that get all the attention. Ninety-nine point, nine, nine, nine have no issues."

That was comforting if you were in the 99 percentile, but the statistic didn't mean a thing for those outside of it. I didn't want my Jessie to be one of the small group of outliers.

I wanted a message sent to the killers and abusers out there; they had to answer to me.

Chapter 20

"Homicide, Detective Luca."

"Hello, Detective. This is Dave McGregor. You came to our house a day ago."

"How are you, Mr. McGregor?"

"Almost over the incident."

"Good. We'll catch whoever did it. What can I do for you?"

"I went to the bank and have the information you wanted on my Patek."

"Oh, thank you. What do you have?"

"Here's the serial number for our family's Calatrava model."

I jotted down the serial number. "I'll do my best in trying to get it back to you."

"It would mean a lot to me. I don't care about the rest of it. They can keep it. But my dad gave that to me, and well, you understand what that means to me."

"I do. Thanks for getting this to me so quickly. As soon as there is a development I can share, I'll call you."

"Hold on a minute, I also have the serial number to my wife's watch that they took. It's an Ebel, nothing too expensive and certainly not a Patek, but I bought it for her on the occasion of our fortieth wedding anniversary."

"How long are the two of you married?"

"Fifty-three years this coming July."

"That's wonderful."

McGregor gave me the serial number for his wife's watch, and I hung up hoping there was a chance I could surprise them by returning their watches. The problem was that stolen goods are rarely recovered. They're usually fenced by the thieves a day or two after they were stolen.

I felt bad for the couple. They were responsible citizens harmlessly living the rest of their lives. Why did those bastards have to pick on them? I knew the answer. It was because they were vulnerable, just like the women and children who were preyed upon by disturbed men.

"Derrick, can you do me a favor."

"Sure. What's up?"

"We have the details of two watches that were stolen from the McGregors. Get this to every pawn shop in the area. Not just Collier, get the info out to the shops in Lee and Charlotte counties, as well."

"I'm on it."

Derrick began sending the hot-goods alert to the area's pawn shops. I thought we had a slim chance of locating the watches and put my attention toward figuring out how to use the MS clue since the first three neurologists I called pulled the privacy curtain down.

***

I took a sip of coffee and opened my email box. Scanning the twenty-five or so that had come in overnight, I saw one that stood out.

The sender was Joyce Wild. That was the same name as the kid that Brian Wild and Jillian Evan's had. It couldn't be. Could it? Why would she send an email to me? I clicked it open:

Dear Detective Frank Luca,

My name is Joyce Wild. My father does not know

I am writing this. I got your email from the card you

gave dad. Please do not tell him I don't want to get in

trouble.

No one is telling me anything about what happened to my mother and who did it.

You are who is in charge, so, I wanted to ask you what is going on and who killed my mom. My grand mom says I have a right to know.

Can you please help me?

Sincerely. Joyce Jill Wild

P.S. Don't tell my dad.

P.P.S. my cell number is 996-500-1021

For some reason, the fact the kid had her mother's name for a middle name jumped out at me. Was that a new thing she'd adopted?

I reread the email.

I wondered what her father had told her. Did the kid know that she was strangled to death? That was a disturbing thing to know. I would shield my kid from information like that.

It felt like her father wasn't concerned about the murder of his ex-wife. He didn't want it to upset their lives. Death, especially a violent death like that of Jillian Evans, was tough for an adult to deal with. I couldn't imagine what a young girl, whose mother was murdered, felt.

I really hoped this kid was able to overcome the fact that her mother had abandoned her due to her illness. I'm sure that the recent attempt by Jillian to gain custody probably confused the girl. But I believed Joyce probably welcomed the opportunity to reunite with her mother, even though the father most likely discouraged it.

What a shame. This poor girl didn't have a mother in her life for years, and then when she does appear, she is murdered. It was a sickening example of how unfair life could be.

An overwhelming need to help this kid came over me. I needed to get some air and headed to the parking lot.

The heat felt good, warming the chill I always had from air-conditioning. Even though I knew the brazen Capital Grille robbery had caused a significant number of people to stay home and was a threat to the town and the way of life I loved, the desire to chase down the killer of this kid's mother was what I wanted and needed to do.

Going to the sheriff was useless. With the pressure he was under, there was no way he'd let me go back to the Evans case. I had to find the Popeye gang and fast. It was the only way we were going to be able to keep the basic underpinnings of our economy intact and for me to get back to what I did best.

Chapter 21

It was time to ask Chester to see if he could deliver on a difficult request. I knew the sheriff, and pressure, real or perceived, was something he didn't respond to well. A phone call was the way to approach this.

"Hello, Sheriff, I hope you're well."

"You going to tell me you have a bead on the Popeye gang?"

"Not quite, but it's about that case."

"Go ahead."

"You generously offered your help yesterday, and I have something you might be able to assist with."

"Get to it, Luca."

Was I beginning to act like Derrick?

"What we could use is help with accessing medical records to help narrow things down. We have the MS patient angle I referred to in my report, and I'd like to focus on it."

"That's a large pool of people."

"I know, sir, but we could quickly thin it out with demographics. But we're going to need subpoenas to do that. We could get lucky, and find a patient with a limp."

"That may be difficult, but if you submit a request, I'll personally see if I can convince a judge to grant it."

"Thank you, sir. You'll have it within the hour."

I hung up. "Finish up the warrant request. Chester is going to see what he can do."

"This is the widest request I've ever been involved with."

"That's why we're basing it on males and ages. Otherwise, Chester or not, we wouldn't stand a chance with a judge. They approve this, we get a list, and zero in on Spanish surnames. Then we go back for another subpoena looking for anyone with a limp."

"I hope it helps catch these bastards. We have to get back to the Evans case before it goes cold."

I wanted to tell Derrick about the email from the victim's daughter. He'd want to know what I was going to do with it, and the fact was, I had no idea.

"Trust me, it's keeping me up at night."

"I'd like to give the bastard who strangled her a bit of their own medicine."

"As soon as we catch this gang, we'll put his ass behind bars for good. Get that request to Chester. One of my contacts gave me a lead on an informant who might have something on the Popeye gang."

***

Ronnie Romero was a deputy with the Lee County Sheriff's Office, and his beat was the high-crime area known as Lehigh Acres. Ronnie was into wine. We'd met two months ago at a wine tasting at Total Wine and hit it right off. There weren't too many cops into wine, but the ones who were had a passion for what we called recycled rainwater.

I pulled into the Winn-Dixie parking lot on Joel Boulevard and hopped into Romero's car. We shook hands.

"Ronnie, how's it going?"

"Not bad. You drink anything good lately?"

"I've been checking out some Sicilian wines. The ones from Mt. Etna are good but getting pricey. There's a grape called frappato that I like. Tastes like red berries."

"Yep, I know it. I think it's best when they blend it with Nero d'Avola. They call it Cerasuolo di Vittoria."

"I like the Nero d'Avola. Is a blend like that expensive?"

"No, even though it's Sicily's only designated and controlled wine."

"It has the DOCG label, like Chianti Classico?"

"Yep, like Barolo, Brunello, and a handful of others."

"I'm gonna check that out, right away, maybe even on the way home."

He wagged a finger at me. "Don't drink and drive, partner."

"Amen. You seeing any impact on restaurant business since this shit happened?"

"Not that I know of. We're running more patrols, but we don't have your swanky joints up here."

"Tell me about your informer."

"Emmanuel Diaz. In the street he goes by the name Ghost."

"Ghost?"

"Was, or probably still is, a meth user. We busted him with a gang doing home invasions. Five or six of them would storm a home. They didn't give a damn who was home, kids or not."

The similarity in style lifted my expectations. "That sounds desperate."

"Not really. They're part of the Jacksonville Blanco gang."

"Jacksonville?"

"Yep, it's not only legit businesses expanding in Florida."

"Can we trust this guy?"

"Age-old question, my friend. He's no different than any other informer."

Informants were an important source for law enforcement, but they were prone to embellishing, if not completely fabricating stories to save their own asses.

"How'd you turn him?"

"He gave up the guys who told them what houses to hit and the fencing operation."

Romero parked just inside a sign that said Lehigh Acres Veteran's Park. Across the road a small crowd was watching a baseball game. We walked toward a lake, and Romero pointed.

"That's Diaz, on the bench."

We were steps away when a cloud of smoke encircled his head. There was no cigarette smell; he was vaping.

The informant was thin, sporting a mop of brown hair and sideburns that were too long. He stood. I didn't get a good feeling from him.

"How you doing, Ghost?"

"All right. What's up?"

"This is a buddy of mine from Collier. He wants to ask you about the Capital Grille robbery."

He shook his head.

I said, "I understand you may know some of the guys who pulled the job."

He shrugged. "Could be."

"How do you know about it?"

"Everybody was talking about it. What they did took balls."

"And somebody opened his mouth to take credit?"

"That's what hit me when I heard it."

"Heard what?"

"This dude was playing nine ball at the next table, and he was shooting off his mouth about how they scared the shit out of everyone. That they stormed the place and made everybody get on the ground and robbed them."

"Did he mention the Capital Grille by name?"

"Not that I heard."

"So, this guy is playing pool, and you overhear him bragging about running into a place, making the people get on the ground and then robbing them?"

"Yeah. That's what I said."

"Who was he telling it to?"

"The guy he was shooting pool with."

"What was his reaction?"

"Like, holy shit, you're a fucking wild man. He couldn't believe it."

"Did the guy have a limp?"

"A limp? No."

"An accent of any kind, maybe Spanish?"

"No."

"Did he say anything specific about anybody they robbed?"

"He was shitting off about some hot motherfucking honey that he wanted to jump on. Said the bitch was wearing a short-assed skirt, and he gave her ass a squeeze."

"He said he touched a woman diner?"

He took a hit on his vape. "Uh-huh."

"Where did you hear this?"

"When we was playing pool."

"Where?"

"The Homestead Pub on Homestead Road."

I turned to Romero. "They have any cameras there?"

"Not that I know of."

The snitch said, "No way. They put in cameras, nobody would go there."

"Okay. Tell me about the man doing the bragging. Do you know him?"

"Not much. I seen him around sometimes."

"You ever work with him?"

"No."

"What's his name?"

"I don't know."

"What does he look like?"

"He's a black dude. About the same height as you but bigger."

"Any scars or tattoos?"

"No, but he got an earring. A gold hoop thing, looks like a girl thing."

"How about his hair?"

"Normal, no 'fro or anything."

"This guy have any history of robbing that you know of?"

"Not that I know, but I mean, you gotta keep your mouth shut. You know what I mean?"

Chapter 22

It was like putting the perimeter of a jigsaw puzzle together. It didn't look like much, but once you had the outside pieces, it was easier to fill in the gaps.

I pulled the Cherokee into a spot out of the sun and hustled into the office. As soon as I took my jacket off, Derrick said, "How'd you do with the snitch?"

"We have a couple of pieces of intel to follow up."

"Great. What did you get?"

"Guy claims one of the thieves was shooting off his mouth in a pool hall. Said the man doing the talking was a black guy, my height but heavier."

"With a limp?"

"No."

"Okay. But even with their Popeye masks, we should be able to determine if one or more of the robbers were black."

"Unless they were wearing hoods."

"A couple were."

"And he said that there was a girl or woman dressed in a short dress that the thief touched on her butt."

"I don't remember anything like that in the witness statements."

"It could be the guy was bragging, or the woman was too embarrassed to say anything."

"We need to reinterview everybody."

"Hold on. There's too many of them. Almost a hundred and fifty. Check the list and focus on the women. Start with anyone in the sixteen-to-fifty age range. We'll at least narrow down the race, and see if this guy is the real deal or not. Of course, any contact made by this thug could be helpful."

"What about trying to bring this guy in?"

"Romero is going to watch the pool hall, and the informant said he'd call him if he saw him. Get started with the witnesses."

"We're going to need help if we get the warrant. There's going to be a ton of people to interview."

"Chester offered to give us help, and we're going to take him up on that as well. Check the list for females. I just had an idea with an outside chance of working."

Where would someone buy eight to ten Popeye masks? I couldn't see any of the party stores stocking that number of masks, especially in March, but I wasn't taking any chances.

I checked with the Party City store on Pine Ridge, and the girl said that hardly anyone bought the old cartoon characters anymore and that they wouldn't stock that many of Popeye even during Halloween season.

It was a long shot that the thieves would have bought them at a retail store as it left a trail. They had to have bought them online. Googling it brought a list of offerings. I went to Amazon. They had clothing and T-shirts with the cartoon character but no masks. The Party City girl was right. If Amazon wasn't selling it, that meant no one wanted it.

eBay was my next selection. Their offerings were a single used mask here and there, and a few vintage masks selling for two hundred bucks each. I wanted to know who was spending that kind of dough on old masks of Popeye but moved on.

I searched the first three pages of results, but besides sailor hats, forearm props, and corncob pipes, there was nothing. No masks. That was weird. I thought you could find anything for sale.

That meant if I could find a seller, it was likely the place the robbers got theirs. Who supplied the masks?

"Frank, there were sixty-seven females at the Capital Grille that night. Thirty-two over fifty years old and nine under sixteen. That leaves me with twenty-six to talk to."

"Start with women twenty to thirty-five years old."

"That really narrows it. I think there's only eight of them."

"Perfect, get moving."

"I'm on it."

"Let me ask you, where do you think this gang bought the Popeye masks?"

"He's an old cartoon guy. I can't see a party supply store having it. Had to be online."

"I checked, nothing on Amazon, eBay, and the costume retailers."

"Um, maybe they went to one of the Chinese internet sellers, like Tmall or JD.com."

As soon as Derrick left, I checked into those sites. I translated their pages into English but came up with nothing. I leaned back in my chair thinking Popeye was out of favor everywhere but in Collier County.

I tried to think of other places to check. Walmart popped into my mind. I knew there was a slim chance they'd carry the masks, so I began tapping my keyboard when an email came in.

It was from Joyce Wild:

Hello Detective Frank Luca,

It's me again.

I didn't hear from you and wanted to make sure you saw my email. Some people, like my dad, don't check email every day. So, I figured to try again in case it went to spam or something.

Please, I want to know what is going on with what happened to my mother.

I hope you are doing something about it. It seems nobody seems to care but me.

You are the only one that I know that can help me.

Please help me.

Thank you,

Joyce Wild

I will give you my cell number again 996-500-1021

I had to hand it to this kid; she was persistent. The way it came through to me was that she wanted justice for her mother. She wasn't going to let it go. I wasn't sure what the protocol was.

We weren't allowed to question a minor without a parent or legal representative unless there was an arrest made. This was a reversal. She wanted to question me. I liked this kid and knew nothing about her. Her mother had put her through a mental ringer, and yet she was pushing for action to solve her murder.

Brian Wild had done a good job raising her. The kid was acting like an adult, taking responsibility for ensuring her mother's case wouldn't wither away. I couldn't blame the kid. It appeared to her that no one else was interested in finding out what happened.

I hoped like hell she wouldn't find out that we were out looking for a gang that robbed restaurants instead of chasing down her mother's killer. I'd have to deal with her sooner or later.

One of my favorite sayings was that there was no time like the present to do something. It was easy to tell someone that but harder to execute. Postponing it would buy me time to nail the robbers and get back to chasing her mother's murderer. It felt like the right thing to do.

The problem was avoiding Joyce Wild would reinforce the feeling that she was alone, that no one cared about her mother's death. I had to give this child a voice, to help her process what had happened by providing a measure of justice.

Chapter 23

Plugging Popeye masks into the search bar of the last major retailer I could find in India yielded nothing. Mary Ann had told me to check Russian and Indonesian sites as well.

It was surprising how many sites came up in Indonesia. When I Googled its population, I had to look twice: two hundred and seventy million. The mostly Muslim nation was just behind America in the number of citizens.

I worked my way to the fifth retail site when Derrick called my cell phone.

"Frank, the second woman I talked to said that there was definitely an African American male in the group of robbers."

"What about the inappropriate touching?"

"Nothing yet."

"Find out what room she was dining in, and check with any other women in that room before going back to the original target set."

"Got it. Any luck with the masks?"

"Nothing. I'm halfway around the world. It's feeling like a waste of time. They'd buy disguises from some Third World country but storm a restaurant during prime time? I don't think so."

"It was a good idea."

"I'm not totally giving up on it yet."

"I'll let you know what I come up with after talking to the rest of the women."

I went through two more sites when the phone rang. It was the sheriff.

"Judge Whitmore rejected the application."

"That's unfortunate, sir."

"There is hope though. I talked to him off the record, and he said we were too ambitious. He suggested focusing on the places we believe this man would have been treated at."

"I see."

"Do you have an idea as to which doctors may have been taking care of him?"

I didn't. "Yes. Let me go through the list, and I'll modify the request."

"Anything else to report?"

"We've got another bead on someone. An informant up in Lehigh Acres said that he overheard a man bragging that he participated in the robbery. The man in question is an African American, midthirties, about five foot ten."

"Do we have any corroboration?"

"Detective Dickson just spoke with a diner who confirmed the race of one of the thieves. He's interviewing others as we speak."

"Shouldn't you be with him?"

"I'm working another angle at the moment, sir."

"Get that amended request to me ASAP."

I pulled out the list of clinics and doctors specializing in neurology. There were forty-five of them. The only thing we knew about the patient was that he was a crook. It was a crapshoot predicting what place someone like him would go to.

Focusing on those that were in or near less desirable neighborhoods, I selected ten physicians. Then I added three that were the largest. It took me forty minutes to create the warrant request. I hand delivered it to the sheriff's secretary and went back downstairs.

Exiting the stairwell, I realized it was going to be a late night. The idea to run by the house, get a dose of Jessie, and give me a chance to see what the nanny was up to, hit me. I checked the time and headed to my office instead. Mary Ann would be leaving for home in half an hour.

What was I going to do about Joyce Wild? I thought about calling her father and telling him that his daughter was advocating for her mother. It wouldn't go over well, I was sure. Who was I to tell him how to bring up his daughter when he seemed to be doing a good job of it? In addition, he was no fan of the mother.

It was the easy way out for me but was the wrong move. In addition, I wondered if it would put a damper on the child's impressive initiative.

I'd have to call her. It couldn't be when her father was around. Pulling up her second email, I sent a brief message asking her when a good time to chat would be.

Seconds later, she responded that 3 p.m. was perfect. Now I had boxed myself in. I had two hours to think over what I was going to say. What was I so nervous about?

***

Crossing over into Bonita Springs, I made a turn at the corner where Bill Smith Appliances had a store and drove down Woods Edge Parkway. A call had come in from Capital Pawn. It looked like they had the Ebel watch stolen from Mildred McGregor.

I pulled up to the green-roofed building and went inside. It was a large store, with departments for jewelry, electronics, musical instruments, tools, and firearms. I couldn't believe how many bicycles they had. Maybe it would be a good place to pick up a bike when Jessie was ready to ride.

A heavily tattooed man was examining a handgun. It looked like a .22 caliber. I kept him in my sight as I made my way to the jewelry counter. They had a bigger display than Macy's. An older woman was behind the counter. Showing my badge, she said that the manager was waiting in his office.

Before following her, I took another look at the firearm customer. He was now holding what looked like a .45, palm side down. No one holds a pistol like that, unless they're in a Hollywood movie about street thugs.

"Detective Luca?"

"Yes."

"Frank Cullen. We spoke on the phone."

We shook hands, and I said, "Thanks for calling about this watch. The sheriff's office appreciates your cooperation."

"Anytime. We have a good relationship with law enforcement and are happy to report anything suspicious."

"Nice to hear. Look, do me favor. There's a customer at the firearms department. He's looking at pistols. Tell the salesperson to be rock certain about him if he's going to buy something."

"If you're concerned, I'll tell her not to sell anything to him."

"It's not my place to tell you who to sell to, but I want buyers of firearms to be vetted like they're marrying your daughter."

"I understand. Excuse me for a moment."

He came back two minutes later. "He's not buying anything today. I told the saleswoman to tell him we had a new corporate policy on handguns that requires a three-day wait period."

"You didn't have to do that."

"It's fine. Now, you were interested in the watch."

"Yes, the Ebel. Do you have it?"

He opened a drawer and took a plastic bag out, handing it to me. I examined the watch; it was the right manufacturer, but that's all I could tell.

"Where's the serial number?"

"It would be on the interior casing."

"Can you open it?"

"Not without damaging it."

"How old do you think this watch is?"

"I don't know much about them, but I fished around the web a little. I'd say it's ten years old, if not older."

McGregor had said he bought it for their fortieth wedding anniversary. He also said they were about to celebrate their fifty-third. At thirteen or so years, the age of the watch fit.

I took several photos and asked, "Who brought this in?"

He flipped open the file on his desk and handed me a copy of a driver's license issued to an Emma Perez. The forty-two-year-old woman lived on East Terry Street in Bonita.

"What was her story?"

"Said her mother had passed away, and she needed the money."

"We're going to need the CCTV footage on her."

He smiled and handed me a thumb drive. "Here you go."

This guy was looking to score points with the police. They bought goods from thieves every day. It was the unspoken fact that led to a constant source of high-margin inventory.

"In the case we're working, time is of the essence. I'd like to see the footage now. Can you pop this in?"

"Absolutely."

I handed the drive back, and he inserted it. It was grainy.

He said, "That's her."

A woman entered the store. She was alone. The time stamp read 7:48 p.m., the night after the robbery. She knew her way around, making a beeline for the jewelry counter.

I watched her take the watch out of her bag and talk with a clerk. They went back and forth before she exchanged the Ebel for an envelope of cash. She stuffed the money in her handbag and strode out of the pawn shop.

"Thanks, I've seen enough."

He gave me the drive, and I said, "I'm going to have to take the watch with me. You can write up a receipt for it, and I'll sign it. If the serial number isn't a match, we'll get it back to you."

Chapter 24

Driving back to the station I was feeling good. We had a solid lead, and it had just been a couple of days. If we could wrap it up quickly, I could get back on the Evans case.

I checked the time. It was 4:27 p.m., an hour and a half past the time I promised to call Joyce Wild. I had reinforced the idea that she couldn't trust adults.

I'd explain everything to her. She'd understand, wouldn't she? First things first. I had to get this watch to the jeweler that the sheriff's office worked with. We had to have confirmation that this belonged to McGregor's wife.

As I weaved through traffic on 41, I marveled at the records kept by the old-timer. It was a practice long gone in our throwaway society. Who bought crazy expensive watches these days?

I nearly ran down a woman when I pulled into Bigham Jewelers parking lot. I grabbed the plastic bag and headed into the store. There were a handful of people being shown what had to be expensive jewelry. The salespeople all spoke in the hushed tones of an undertaker. I asked where the repairs were handled and was pointed toward the back.

At the rear of the store were three service windows. For jewelry? What kind of business was this place doing? I slid my badge and the watch across the ledge and told the jeweler I needed to verify the serial number.

Stepping outside, I called Mary Ann.

"How are you doing?"

"Good. Where are you?"

"At a jewelry store, but don't get your hopes high. I'm having a serial number checked on a stolen watch. Besides, with the prices in here, I could buy a car."

"What store is that?"

"Bigham."

"Figures."

"How's Jessie doing?"

"She's walking around touching everything. We wanted her to walk, and now I get to follow her around, or she's either going to get hurt or break something."

"She's amazing."

"You should have seen her when I came home. Jimena was reading to her, and when she was leaving, Jessica started crying. She didn't want her to go. She was holding on to her pants. It was hilarious."

Just what I was afraid of. What was coming next, that she would rather be with the nanny than me?

"She might be getting too attached to her."

"There's nothing wrong with that. I don't feel half as guilty leaving her. Jessica is in good hands with her."

"I don't know what time I'm going to get home. Don't wait on dinner for me."

"Make sure you get home before she goes to bed."

"Don't worry. She won't be able to go to sleep if I don't read to her."

"Let me go, Frank. Jessica is heading into our bedroom."

"I'll see you later."

I stood in the sun for a moment before going back in. A woman had actually bought something and was checking out. I wondered how much she'd spent; maybe I should escort the lady to her car.

The jeweler was behind his workstation. I knocked on the wall. He lifted his head, grabbed the watch and came to the window.

"Here you go." He passed the watch and a slip of paper across the counter.

"Thank you." I jotted a note on the rear of my card. "Here's my card. Send your bill in with it."

I looked at the serial number as I dug into my pocket. I compared the two numbers. It was a match. We had the stolen watch and the woman who had pawned it.

We were closing in. I'd be able to finally get back to the Evans murder. I took my phone out. I felt like calling Joyce Wild but decided against it. It would be better to focus my energies on wrapping up the robbery.

"Derrick, the watch is the one stolen in Cote d'Azur's parking lot."

"Sweet. Where are you?"

"Coming in. Get McQuire to provide two unmarked cars to come along with us. I don't know what we're going to find when we go to grab this Perez woman."

"You think that's enough? If the whole gang happens to be there, we'll be outnumbered."

"You're right, make it three cars and us. We'll be fine."

"Got it."

"I'll see you in twenty minutes."

"All right."

"Hey, pull down a map of the area and of her house and make sketches. We need to know what we're dealing with."

***

Six officers filed into our office, cramping the space. Derrick handed copies of what he'd drawn. Emma Perez lived in the center of a small enclave of yellow cinder-block homes. There were six buildings arranged in a semicircle. Each structure contained two apartments.

"Derrick and I are going to Perez's front door. We'll need side and rear coverage. As you can see on the sketch, the target is in the center of a couple of buildings. It's possible other gang members are holed up in one or more of the other units."

Derrick said, "There are at least eight of them in the gang."

I said, "As a precaution, I'd like one on each side and two in the rear of the target. The last three of you should stay back, just off the street, spread out, twenty-five feet or so. Keep your eyes open."

Derrick said, "Everybody got it?"

Heads bobbed in unison, and I said, "I don't want to hear about the heat. Make sure your vests are on before we leave the parking lot. Come on, let's get this done."

We filed into the parking lot. Derrick opened the back of the Cherokee and handed me a vest. I began unhooking the Velcro straps.

Derrick said, "You okay?"

"Yeah, all is good. I just want to get moving."

Every time I strapped protection on, I thought of the danger I was placing myself in. But ever since Jessie was born, before a confrontation, it was taking longer and longer for the uncomfortable feeling to melt away.

The cowboy in most men waned if they'd been hurt, when they got married, or as they aged. For me, it was becoming a father that made me cautious, turning my mortality into reality.

Everyone was dressed and in their cars. Derrick turned out of the parking lot, and the procession was in tow.

I slammed my palm on the dashboard. "Shit!"

"What's the matter?"

"I forgot to call the Lee County Sheriff's Office and tell them we were going on their turf."

"No worries, partner. I called them."

I thanked him but was upset at forgetting something so fundamental. I pushed my regret about chemo brain out of my mind and tried to pump myself up about the arrest we were going to make.

Chapter 25

I pulled down the sun visor as we turned onto East Terry Street. We stopped in front of the one-story, cinder-block property that Emma Perez called home. Two kids were pedaling in a circle in front of the yellow building.

I never liked it when kids were around. There was always the threat of someone getting hurt, but what also bothered me was what went through a child's mind when they saw an adult they knew get arrested.

I opened the Cherokee's door and was greeted with the sound of Spanish music. The guy working on a car two buildings down must have been hard of hearing.

"Let's go, but get those kids out of harm's way."

We trotted across what passed for a lawn as the others fanned out. Derrick handed the kids off to an officer who was laying back. As he jogged to the front door, I rang the bell.

A boy under eight years of age pulled open the door. I wanted to call the entire thing off.

"Hello, young man. Is your mother home?"

I smelled onions frying as he looked at Derrick, then at me. "You want her?"

"Yes, please."

Barefoot, he scampered off calling for his mother. A woman with a baseball cap and kitchen towel in her hands stepped into view. A second later, a little girl on her hands and knees crawled after her. Another complication.

"Emma Perez?"

"Yes. What is it?"

I pulled my badge out. "We're with the Collier County Sheriff's Office."

"Did something happen to Pedro?"

She seemed genuinely surprised. "No, ma'am. Would you mind stepping outside, please?"

Perez turned around. "I'll be right there. Behave yourselves, or no cookies for snack time."

Thieves had snack time as well? The bad feeling I had when we pulled up intensified. Something about this woman was off. She didn't move anything like the woman in the pawn shop video.

She stood in front of her open door. Derrick said, "Where did you get the Ebel watch that you pawned at Capital Pawn?"

"Pawn? I don't know what you're talking about."

"We have you selling a watch to Capital Pawn. It's on video."

"That's impossible. I've never even been in one of those places."

"That's funny, because your license was used as identification for the sale."

She smiled. "My license was stolen a week ago."

I said, "Did you report it missing?"

"Yes. I went down to the DMV and got a new one the same day."

"And that was last Friday?"

"Yes."

"Hang on a second."

I pulled Derrick aside. "Didn't I ask you to check on that?"

"I did. They said it wasn't reported stolen."

"If this is some kind of paperwork screwup, I'm going to lose it."

"Let me call them again."

I went back to Perez, who was now holding her young daughter. "How old is she?"

"Nine months."

"She's cute. My daughter is fourteen months old."

"You're running after her, then."

"You got that right. Where was your wallet stolen?"

"I was shopping at the Winn-Dixie store on Bonita Beach Road. You can check with them; I reported it to them also."

Though I didn't need it, Derrick confirmed that Lee County had just updated the license records. This woman was not the person who sold the watch to Capital Pawn.

The woman's son came to the door as I said, "I'm sorry for the inconvenience, ma'am, but it looks like the county mixed up the paperwork."

"I understand."

"Hold on a minute."

I jogged to the Cherokee and grabbed a plastic badge out of the community policing bag.

"Here you are, young man. You're a deputy now."

The boy tried to clip it to his T-shirt, and his mother said, "What do you say?"

"Thank you."

"You're welcome. Keep your eyes open and report any trouble."

"I will."

"And make sure you take care of your mother."

***

As soon as Derrick got behind the wheel, he said, "Jesus. Was that embarrassing or what?"

"No doubt. It could have been worse if the Lee sheriff had sent a car out."

"It'd take us a year to live that down."

"How the hell can they issue a new license and not update the records? I thought it was all digital."

"The guy at the DMV said they were moving everything over to the new state system."

"Does anybody understand how much time they're costing us? Chester's breathing down my neck, and we have to deal with crap like this."

"I thought we had something."

"We do. We have a woman who looks something like Emma Perez. We just have to find her. I want to get pictures made from the pawn shop video and circulate them."

"We might get lucky."

"I'm betting that the woman who pawned the watch is the same one who stole Perez's license."

"You want the surveillance video from Winn-Dixie, right?"

"Absolutely, for last Friday. Let's see if we can find her entering and if she was with anyone."

"Maybe she lives in the neighborhood."

"I don't know. It would be risky to steal in a place where people know you."

"True, but anything is possible."

"You said a mouthful."

My cell phone vibrated. It was the sheriff.

"Hello, sir."

"How did it go?"

"It wasn't her. They had stolen her identity and used her license to pawn it."

He exhaled. "Okay, let's move forward. I was able to get Judge Whitmore to grant the medical records subpoena."

"Excellent, sir. We really appreciate your help with that."

"Don't make it go to waste. I want them caught—now."

Before I finished saying, "I understand, sir"—the line went dead.

Chapter 26

The last two cups of coffee had zero effect on my energy or my mood. I leaned back in my chair, knowing it would take considerable time to weed through the medical records. There were bound to be scores of them, and that was just the starting point. After we slimmed it down, we'd have to try to identify who had a limp. It sounded easy, but doing it would require another warrant.

It was almost six thirty, and I was still at my desk. The thought that it was too late to call Joyce Wild added to my depressed state of mind. To make matters worse, I hadn't seen my daughter awake for two nights in a row. If I didn't get my ass moving, it'd be three.

A text came in from Mary Ann. The woman had a sixth sense. She'd sent a picture of Jessie in her pajamas. It was great shot of her smiling. I wasn't into going back and forth with a million texts and called her.

"Hey, that was a nice shot. I'm gonna make it my screen saver."

"Are you on the way home?"

"Not yet, just wrapping things up."

"You better hurry."

"I will. Put her on the phone, I need to hear her."

"Hey, Jessie. It's Daddy."

A line of gibberish featuring a couple of dadas lifted my mood. I told Mary Ann I'd be home in half an hour and hung up.

It was time to go. As I grabbed my jacket my cell rang. It was my Lee County cop-and-wine-drinking buddy.

"Hey, Ronnie, how is it going?"

"Good, Frank. Look, that snitch Diaz, he just called. He said the guy who was bragging about robbing the Capital Grille is back playing pool at the Homestead."

"He's sure it's him?"

"That's what he said."

"Can you trust him?"

"You know what we're dealing with, but he doesn't have a reason to lie. I told him you'd meet him there."

"I'm on my way. You going to meet me?"

"Wish I could, bro, but it's Jeanette's birthday, and you know where that would put me?"

"She wouldn't let you buy another bottle of wine."

"Amen."

"Tell her happy birthday, and buy a good wine to celebrate, you cheapskate."

***

The Homestead Sports Pub was one of several small businesses in an aging strip center. Pushing through the glass door, I was greeted with the smell of stale beer. A guitarist was setting up on a small stage to the right. Opposite, a half a dozen people were drinking at the bar. One of them was Diaz.

We made eye contact. He took a sip of beer and headed toward the bathroom. My shoes were sticking to the tile floor as I followed him.

He was standing at the urinal. I checked the stall; it was empty, and I went to the sink. Turning the water on, I asked, "Where is he?"

"Playing the table to the right. He's wearing jeans with a chain hanging and a Jedi T-shirt."

I nodded.

"Don't say anything about me. I'm outta here."

I went to the bar and thought about ordering a glass of wine before remembering where I was. Yellowtail by the barrel would be better than whatever they were serving.

Sipping my club soda, I observed the man I was here to see. He was leaning over the table, stroking his stick as he prepared to strike the cue ball. Just before sending the ball on its way, he looked up in my direction.

Our eyes met for a second. He went back to his game, but I knew he'd pinned me for a cop. The criminal element had an uncanny ability to detect the law. I didn't care. He wasn't getting out of here without talking to me.

I put my glass down and headed over. He knew I was coming, but he picked a piece of chalk and applied it to the tip of his cue.

"I'd like to talk to you. You want to step outside?"

"You're a cop, ain't you?"

"Detective Luca, Collier County Sheriff's Office. You want to see my badge?"

He shook his head and leaned his stick against the wall. He told his friend to play out the rack and said, "What do you want with me?"

He was wearing a Rolex. Spoils from another robbery?

"If you want to talk in front of everyone, it's fine with me."

He backed up a few feet and leaned against the wall.

"Ask your questions."

"What's your name?"

"Jamal Washington."

"Let me see your driver's license."

"I don't think I have to show you that."

"Either here or at the station. Your call."

He dug out his wallet and handed me his ID. It was his real name, and he lived on Sunshine Boulevard South.

"What do you do for a living?"

"I'm between jobs now."

"What did you do?"

"Worked at Baer's Furniture."

"Pay must have been pretty good there."

"Bullshit, just over minimum wage, and they work you like a dog. That's why I left."

"Nice watch. Where'd you get something like that, working at Baer's?"

"It's a knockoff, man."

"Looks good. What did it cost you?"

"Forty bucks."

"You have any friends with MS?"

He looked like I'd asked him for the meaning of life.

"What? You mean that disease where they can't walk and stuff?"

"Multiple Sclerosis. It's an autoimmune illness that affects the brain and spine."

"Shit's nasty."

"Do you know anyone with it?"

"Nah, I seen some people. Last place I lived, a guy had it."

"Where was that?"

"Kingston Arms, in Cape Coral."

"How long you been down here?"

"About a year."

"You have a record?"

He shrugged.

"You can tell me, or I can look it up."

"Breaking and entering."

There was one thing that fit. "Serve any time?"

"Eight months."

Long enough to further his criminal education, but more importantly, jail was the perfect place to meet coconspirators. Crimes too numerous to count were hatched behind bars.

"You know anyone involved in the Capital Grille robbery?"

"Me? No idea who did it."

"That's funny you say that. We have a witness who said you were bragging that you were involved in it."

"Who the fuck say something like that?"

"Can't say."

"That's bullshit."

"Were you part of the crew that pulled that job?"

"No."

"Then why did you say you were?"

He shrugged. "Asshole I was shooting nine ball with was giving me a bunch of shit about how tough he was, and I just made it up."

"Why'd you do something like that?"

"I don't know; I just did."

"You said something about touching one of the women that was robbed that night. So, you made that up too?"

"Look, man, the guy was a jerk off. I was playing with him. I'd never do that, man. I got too much respect for women."

I'd find out if that was true or not, along with everything else he said. We had a name and an address. We'd put together a profile and put some eyes on this guy.

Chapter 27

I left the bar continuing to feel like I was spinning my wheels. I knew that solving a crime wasn't like taking an express elevator to the top. It was trudging up the stairs, one at a time.

Knowing that didn't make me feel better. There'd been minuscule progress on the Capital Grille robbery, and the Evans case was sitting on the shelf. I was a damn homicide detective. I made my living catching killers, not chasing down thieves.

I put together a surveillance request on Jamal Washington. At least I didn't have to worry about Chester approving it. With his focus on the robbery, he'd go overboard in tailing this possible suspect.

It was late, and Jessie would be sleeping by the time I got home. I might as well try to get something accomplished to avoid another wasted day. I'd lost whatever momentum we'd had in the Evans case. I needed to reconnect with it, or it would go cold, and I'd never be able to give Joyce Wild an answer as to who murdered her mother, and why.

Opening the credenza's top drawer, I pulled out the Evans case file. The to-do list was formidable, but there was that boyfriend of Jillian Evans that we'd just found out about before we were pulled off the case. His name was Barry Eisner.

We needed background information on this man. Finding out where he lived and worked was straightforward. I pulled up his DMV record for his address and used the state system to learn that Eisner was employed by a roofing company. He had to be busy; the hurricane two years ago took a toll on roofs nearing replacement age.

It was time to look into the Collier's record management system. It was a useful tool that recorded every interaction between the police and a person. You didn't have to get arrested to be in the system: a car accident where the cops were called or if you called 911 would put it on record.

What I discovered was troubling.

***

It was after ten by the time I walked in the door. Mary Ann was on the couch watching a movie. It was one of those Hallmark movies where life was perfect, and a crime was when someone stole grandma's apple pie.

"Sorry, it was a crazy day."

"Your dinner is sitting on the stove."

"Thanks, I'm going to check on Jessie."

"Don't you dare wake her up."

I stared at my daughter for a couple of minutes. She was precious. I changed and went back into the family room.

"She's sleeping like a rock."

"Of course she is, it's almost ten thirty."

I took the tin foil off my dinner plate.

The turkey burger was as cold as Mary Ann. I ate it anyway. I was dead tired and needed a boost. I grabbed a bag of pretzels and sat down in my recliner and tried to break the cold front.

"You're eating pretzels at this hour?"

"Just going to have a few."

"You wanted to lose a couple of pounds, didn't you? You eat those pretzels now, you're really wasting calories."

She was right. Five or six pounds needed to come off my midsection. Even though I felt like I deserved it after the day I had, I put the bag on the table. "How was your day?"

"Okay."

"What's the matter?"

"You said you weren't going to do this anymore."

"Do what?"

"Don't play dumb, Frank. You promised to be home for dinner every night, to be here to spend time with Jessica."

"It's crazy. You don't know what we're up against. Chester is barking up my ass and—"

"If it's not one thing, it'll be something else."

"The Capital Grille robbery could kill tourism. These guys hit another restaurant, and the town will die. I would've made it tonight, but I had to check out a suspect in Lee."

"Look, I understand every now and then things heat up, but this is three nights in a row. You want her to start thinking you're a stranger?"

"I'm sorry, Mary Ann, really I am. It won't happen again."

"Okay. What happened up in Lee?"

"One of Ronnie Romero's informants overheard this guy bragging about his role in the Capital Grille robbery. He needs checking out, but I think he was just shooting his mouth off. For whatever deranged reason, these punks are looking for what they call 'street cred,' and it could be that's what this clown was doing."

"Another washout?"

"Looks that way, but at least I uncovered something that could be big on the Evans murder."

"I thought Chester told you to stay off that until the robbery was solved."

"He did, but here's the thing. You know that the longer it goes, the colder it gets. And the woman's kid sent me an email."

"She did?"

"Not one but two."

"You have to be careful with stuff like that, Frank. What did you do?"

"Nothing yet. But the poor kid is looking for answers on her mother's death, and her father, who was in the middle of a custody battle with the mother, doesn't seem to give a damn."

"So, it's up to you?"

I shrugged. "I feel for the kid. She's confused. I don't want her feeling she can't rely on anyone."

"That's not your role. She has a father, Frank."

"I know. I'm just trying to—"

"You used to tell me all the time, 'Leave your emotions home.' Heed your own advice. I'm going to bed."

"I want to watch the news. I just ate and don't want to lie down yet."

The weather was on, again. It's Southwest Florida. It's going to be sunny and hot. As the weather gal droned on about possible rain showers in tomorrow's forecast, my cell vibrated.

It was the sheriff. Had he read the log and knew I had gone to Lehigh Acres to interview Washington? I thought about what to say.

"Hello, Sheriff."

"They struck another restaurant."

I didn't have to ask who. "Where, sir?"

"Fort Myers. A place called Harold's, on Forty-One."

Wearing a blue nightie, Mary Ann came out of the bedroom. "Who are you talking to at this hour?"

I put a finger to my lips. "What time?"

"Eight thirty or so. I need you to get up there."

"I'm on my way, sir."

I hung up and turned to my wife. "Sorry, babe, these bastards stormed another restaurant in Fort Myers. The sheriff wants me to go to the scene."

Was Jamal Washington laughing at me? Did he finish his pool game, join the other thugs and hit Harold's? If he did, he'd rival some of the most audacious criminals I'd ever encountered.

He had more than enough time to do it, but wouldn't the gang meet up beforehand to go over their plans? Out playing pool before committing armed robbery?

It didn't fit. Or did it?

Chapter 28

Even though I'd been up most of the night, I made sure to be at the office before Derrick. I had left him a note that I was meeting with Chester, and when that ended, rode the elevator down to my office.

Derrick said, "Man, you look shot, Frank."

"I didn't get home until almost three in the morning."

"You should have called me. I would have liked to have been there."

"I knew you and Lynn went to the tasting for your wedding. Besides, there's no sense in having both our asses dragging."

"I know you were looking out for me, but I want to be there. It's the only way I'm going to be half as good as you."

My results were no better than his at the moment, and the way I was running into walls, Chester would have him running things before I knew it. "You're doing fine. How'd it go with the venue?"

"The food was good. I just think they give you better food to taste than they serve for the wedding. Anyway, we tied up all the loose ends with them. Everything is set."

"We're looking forward to helping you guys celebrate."

"I want to see your ass up dancing."

"We'll see about that. Let's get in gear and catch these bastards. Chester got a pair of cars with eyes on Washington. It seems crazy that he'd be involved in this, but he has a longer record than he said, and though it's mostly low-level crap, we have to consider the possibility."

"If he told the gang you went to see him, they would have canceled their plans."

"You'd think so. Here's what we know about last night's crime."

I told him there was no doubt it was the same gang. Eight people wearing Popeye masks stormed Harold's Restaurant. The high-end eatery was considered the best place to eat in Fort Myers.

The fine dining establishment, located in a strip center on Route 41, was significantly smaller than the Capital Grille. There were fifty-three diners in its sole dining room.

In a small twist, they took whatever money was in the cash register, along with stripping the patrons of their jewelry and cash.

With everyone in one room, we were able to get a bit more detail on the gang members. The consensus was three of the robbers were black, two had Spanish accents, and the others were believed to be white.

The one guy we knew the most about, Mr. Limp, wasn't there. That was disappointing. Was he too ill to participate? An interesting observation by several diners was that one of the robbers was female.

The gang had used another stolen van, blue this time, dumping it in the Walmart parking lot on Six Mile Cypress Parkway. An employee on the retailer's loading dock saw the gang transfer into a Japanese SUV.

The warehouse worker was too far away to describe any of them but said he saw one of them reach to the back of their head and release a bun or ponytail. He couldn't distinguish whether it was a woman or a male with long hair.

"These guys are reckless, Frank."

"On the surface, I agree. But they did change it up by going into Fort Myers and by targeting a smaller restaurant, cutting down the risk factor."

"They're going to make a mistake."

"Let's hope it doesn't cost anyone their life when they do."

"You think they'll hurt someone?"

"They're armed. Anything can happen, especially if someone panics."

"That would be a disaster. Nobody would eat out."

"I don't need the reminder after speaking to Chester. He's going to hold a news conference this afternoon to try and get ahead of the news flow."

"Good luck with that."

"I know. We keep our heads down, we'll get these bastards. I want to start with the Winn-Dixie video."

***

The grocery store footage rolled on. "Freeze it, Derrick. I think that's her."

"Let me blow it up."

"That's her."

Emma Perez was pushing an empty shopping cart into the entrance. Before the sliding doors closed behind her, a gray Honda SUV pulled up. A woman jumped out of the passenger seat and headed into the store. The vehicle pulled out of sight.

There was something about the way this woman walked. "I'm getting the feeling that woman is the one who pawned the watch."

"Why is that?"

"The way she moves. Keep watching."

As the video played, I wondered whether it was also the same woman who'd stolen Perez's wallet. Ten minutes passed, and the woman came out. She had no bags.

She stepped to the curb, and the gray Honda pulled up. The woman hopped in, and the car took off.

"That had to be her. She didn't buy anything."

I thought it was her as well but had to temper things. We had zero evidence. "Maybe she went in looking for something they didn't have. She could have gone into the pharmacy and stuck the meds in her bag."

"Come on, you kidding me?"

"Zero in on the car. See if we can pick up the plate number."

The problem was Florida only required a rear plate, and we had no footage of the back of the SUV. We had clean shots of the side of the car but only a partial of the plate as it pulled away.

"Bring this down to the lab. See if they can work magic and squeeze out the rest of this number. I can't see how, but you never know. And I want pictures of this woman. We need them cleaned up and enlarged. Then we'll compare it to the pawn shop images."

Between Collier and Lee Counties, we had a million cars on the road. I tried to calculate how many gray Honda Pilot SUVs there could be. It had to be a couple of thousand. We'd narrow it down with a partial plate, but it would still be at least a hundred vehicles to sort through.

We could work through that number quickly if the driver and registration matched. We'd weed out by age and gender. The possibility gave me zero comfort. There were more holes than a golf course. Was the vehicle registered in another county? Was the woman even the one who stole the wallet? Had the vehicle been borrowed or stolen?

It was nothing, but it was something to work. We did have the pictures from the pawn shop and now the grocery store. If it was one and the same woman, we'd have something. And there was the tail on Jamal Washington. If he was involved, the tail would produce evidence to act on.

Chapter 29

As the lead detective, the sheriff wanted me in the room. It was more for protocol than for need. The chances he'd ask me to say anything or answer a question were slim.

I watched as he addressed the media. There were more reporters in the room than for any of the homicides we worked. It could have been the brazen way the robberies were committed, but I believed it was the hit to tourism that brought them out.

Did they get the irony of their reporting? I'm not in favor of suppressing news about a crime, but overplaying the threat to tourism would be self-fulfilling.

It was akin to what was done with the coverage of the red tide that plagued the area months after Hurricane Irma hit. It was a serious situation and in need of a permanent solution, but the coverage stuck in people's minds, and though the algae disappeared, tourist bookings were down the following year.

Chester was comfortable behind a podium, more so than in a one-on-one situation. After reading his statement, he fielded a couple of questions like a politician, downplaying but acknowledging the situation while offering words that were meaningless and self-serving.

The sheriff ended the conference and left through a door behind the lectern as reporters fired questions. I slipped out of the room, and heading back to my office, wondered how the papers and TV news would play it.

I checked with the lieutenant running the Washington surveillance, but there was nothing to report. Jamal had left his apartment for a brief period, going to a 7-Eleven before returning home alone. It was ten minutes to three. We had eyes on him for six hours. He hadn't had a visitor, but I would expect gang members to lie low for a day or two after committing a crime.

Derrick was collecting medical records and sent me a text that the lab would have the pictures of the woman in the video ready by four o'clock. He also said that DMV was in the process of running the plate and vehicle combination.

There was an hour or so to pursue what I wanted. As soon as the lab and the DMV produced, I'd be running those threads down. There was an itch that I couldn't put off scratching any longer. I shut the door and picked up the phone.

"Joyce Wild?"

"Yes."

"This is Detective Frank Luca."

"Oh, oh, thanks so much for calling me."

"Is this a good time to talk?"

"Yes, it's perfect."

"I know you're concerned about your mother's case, but I have to notify you that I am not able to discuss the case. It's against department rules."

"I want to know, like, what's going on with what happened and all. Nobody tells me anything. It makes me mad."

"I understand your frustration. I really do, but I can tell you that we're working hard at finding who did this to your mother."

"I hope so. Daddy says not to expect much, that after a while, that the police have so many things to do, that if they don't catch the man fast, that they go to do other things."

"It's true that we're busy, but I promise you that I will not forget about your mother. I'll bring the murderer to justice."

"Daddy says you wasted time by seeing if he did it. He would never do something like that. How can you think he did?"

If anyone wasted time it was her father, who continually lied about his alibi. "We never said he was involved, but part of the process of solving these types of things is to look at everyone who knew your mother. That way we can eliminate as many people as possible. Does that make sense?"

"I, I don't know how you can think that about my father. He's amazing. I mean, sometimes he can be hard, but I guess he has to. You know what I mean?"

It was nice that she was defending her dad. "Yes, I'm sure whatever he does is in your best interests."

"He's been taking care of me my whole life. And I know my mom got sick and all, and he was mad about everything that happened when I was little, but Mom was trying to make up for it. He didn't like it, I know, but he doesn't know what it was like not to have a mom to talk to and everything. I'm like, the only girl in my class without a mom. I mean, there are a couple of girls, like, with no father, but they have a mom. I wish she was still here."

Her voice cracked, and I had to clear my throat, otherwise my voice would be worse than hers.

"I'm very sorry that this happened. Your mother would be proud of you, knowing how much you cared for her and how hard you are trying to see that justice is done."

"You really think so?"

"No doubt about it. The fact that you are seeking information about the case impressed me."

"It's no big deal. I just want to, have to, know what happened, and why."

I had to be careful. Sometimes you can solve a homicide but never find out exactly what actually happened.

"I promise you that I will bring the person who did this to justice."

"How long until you catch them?"

"All I can say at this point is that we've made good progress."

"Oh my God. Really? You're close to catching them?"

"I can't say any more."

"I keep trying to think who did it."

"Is there anything you want to tell me?"

"Just that she was sorry, real sorry, about her getting sick and everything, and that she couldn't help what happened, and that she was going make it up to me. She was starting fresh, you know."

"Everything I have learned about your mother tells me she was a special person. I'm sorry that you have to deal with all this. Please try and hang in there, and remember you have a great dad, who will always be there for you."

"I know, but I wish she was here."

"I've got to get back to work on your mother's case. It was nice talking with you. Take care of yourself, Joyce."

"Who's going let me know what's going on? Can you do it?"

"I'm sorry, but that's something I don't do."

"Please. Can't you just let me know? I won't tell nobody. Please, help me."

"Okay."

"Oh, thank you, thank you. Nanny said the police have all kinds of new technology to help them."

"We do. Look, I really got to get back to finding who did this to your mother."

Chapter 30

Even though my pee-pee alarm hadn't rung, I knew that after three cups of coffee it was time to relieve myself.

"Derrick, I'm heading to the john. Follow up on the DMV records. They promised them yesterday."

"I'm on it."

Just before stepping into the hallway, I said, "And give McQuire a shout. See what's going on with the tail on Jamal. He hasn't gone anywhere but to pick up food."

"You got it."

I slid into a stall and sat. Recently, gently rubbing the long scar that ran across my abdomen was helping to get a flow started. As I tickled the area, I thought about the Evans murder, quickly forcing it out of my head. We had to get the robbery gang first. What did we have?

The woman who pawned McGregor's watch, and the one who followed Emma Perez into Winn-Dixie were one and the same. The question was, who was she?

Photos of her were distributed to frontline officers in both Collier and Lee Counties. Informers were being leaned on to see if they could identify the woman. But the best shot at finding out who she was would come from the public.

The pictures of the mystery woman were being shared with local newspapers, and we had promises from three TV stations to run the picture with a confidential hotline number. Chester tossed around the idea of offering a reward, but I was able to convince him that, though it

122

was a good idea, it would train the public to help only in exchange for cash, an exceedingly dangerous precedent.

I was always amazed when ordinary citizens would step forward with crucial information. Sometimes it would be a family member who'd put aside their loyalty in order to help. There were good people out there. I just wished there were more of them. If there were, I'd have less anxiety about the world Jessie was going to have to navigate.

Assistance from the public was something I looked forward to. However, I dreaded the scores of calls that would inevitably come in from crackpots and lonely old people.

You would think it would be easy to wade through the leads, focusing on those that sounded credible. No doubt, some could be discarded. There were the habitual callers, people with unsound minds, and psychics, which we'd put aside, but besides those, I'd learned we had to follow every lead.

Washing up, I felt a surge of optimism. There was work to be done, but the seeds had been planted.

Derrick hung up the phone as I walked back in. He said, "Jamal is on the move."

"Where to?"

"He's heading north on Forty-One."

"All right, let's see where he ends up. What did the DMV say?"

"We'll have it in ten."

"Any idea how large a list?"

"They didn't say."

Derrick's phone rang. He answered it and jumped to his feet as he hung up.

"Jamal pulled into a Home Depot parking lot and met up with two other cars there."

"It could be the gang. Does McQuire know to look out for someone with a limp? And the woman we're looking for?"

Derrick shrugged as he picked up the phone. "I'll let him know again, just to be sure."

Something I should have done but had never entered my mind was to check the national database for any hits on Barry Eisner. When the idea hit me last night, I slipped out of bed and wrote a note to do that. It was another memory lapse I attributed to chemo brain.

We knew Eisner had a record, but you never knew what some clerk could have misfiled or forgotten to upload. Especially in light of Lee County's DMV screwup, it made sense to be vigilant.

As I opened the national portal, Derrick said, "McQuire said there doesn't seem to be anyone with a limp. But there's two women."

"Tell him to get photos, and send them to us. The woman we're looking for could be there. If she is, we've got them."

For some reason, I still didn't think Jamal was involved. Maybe I was protecting myself by believing that. The alternative, that my gut had failed to signal me, would make me question everything, going forward. It would be professional hell.

There wasn't anything else on Eisner. I was thankful my forgetfulness hadn't been pricey. Though the search hadn't elevated his suspect status, he was up at the top with George Evans.

Derrick said, "Just got the DMV spreadsheet. I'll forward a copy."

It took them time to get it to us, but they had broken down the registration data into columns. In addition to the county, we had info on male and female owners, the year of each vehicle, and the age and race of the registrant. The problem was there were 987 gray Honda Pilots on the list.

We needed to whittle this list and fast.

"How good are you with Excel?"

"I'm not an expert, but I know my way around it. What do you want to do?"

"In the Winn-Dixie video, the vehicle was a late-model one. It was five years old, tops. Anything older had a different front grille and headlights. Can you sort it by the year?"

He came around my desk and tapped away. Thirty seconds later he said, "It's sorted by the year now."

"Good, now let's focus on white male owners, those between twenty-two and forty years of age."

A handful of keystrokes later we had a list that numbered 361.

"Chances are these guys are from Lee, don't you think?"

"Probably." He tapped a couple of keys. "Here we are."

There were 273 names. We'd knocked off three quarters of the list, but we had no way to know if the driver of the Honda was also the owner. We had to tackle the list, but were we going down a rabbit hole?

"We have a profile of the driver. We need to start pulling up each of these guy's driver's license and compare pictures."

"Frank, McQuire just sent in the pictures of the women Jamal Washington is meeting with. Take a look at this."

Chapter 31

I studied the women, discounting the one with a skull tattoo that ran up her neck. Derrick said, "What do you think?"

"I don't know. There's a resemblance, but I don't think it's the same woman."

"Me either."

"Tell McQuire to have a unit approach. Give them a story about an Amber Alert, and get everyone who is there to provide ID. Tell him to run the info. You never know what we'll get on any of them, and we'll know who they are."

"On it."

I didn't like harassing citizens, but it felt like at least one person in that crowd was up to no good. They weren't at a Home Depot for a DIY project. It was a delicate balance between a police state, where people innocently going about their lives could be confronted by an overzealous police force, and acting on intelligence.

There was more than enough solace in knowing that Washington hung out with criminals and had openly bragged at participating in a robbery. Like it or not, I was of the opinion that society had a right to keep a closer eye on those who had been convicted of a crime. And as long as I could back up that belief with a fact or a premonition, it wouldn't keep me up at night.

Putting the first name on the spreadsheet into the driver's license database, I was greeted by a spinning wheel. I groaned. It took a good forty seconds to load. At this rate, Jessie would be shopping for prom dresses before I'd get to the end of the list.

The smiling face of a twenty-eight-year-old was too chubby to be the Winn-Dixie driver. Unless he'd recently lost weight. Nah, I went to the second name on the list and typed it in the search bar.

What was going on? The spinning circle again.

"Derrick, you having problems accessing the DL database?"

"I didn't try yet. What's the matter?"

"It's slow as shit. Maybe there's a problem with it."

"Could be a bandwidth issue."

An image of a thirty-one-year-old man, with a dark complexion, appeared as I said, "Just great." He looked nothing like the target, and I moved on. The name of the next man was the same as the man who'd been on my mind the last two days: Barry Eisner.

What was I doing chasing down robbers when a murderer was on the loose? I knew the financial damage this gang could inflict would be devastating, but what price was higher than the loss of a life?

My skill set was catching killers. Scared diners could weigh the risks of going out to eat. It was a luxury someone dead didn't have. I couldn't do this anymore. I popped out of my chair.

"Derrick, I'll be back in a while. Something has come up."

"Is everything okay?"

"Yeah, no worries."

"Are you sure? There's nothing going on with Jessica, is there?"

He really gave a damn about me. I closed the door. "I didn't want to tell you because I don't want you mixed up in going against Chester."

"Mixed up in what?"

"He wants us to only work on the robbery. I, I can't sit by when a woman has been strangled to death. The case is gonna go cold. We owe it to her family. She has a little girl, for Chrissakes. The kid wants to know what happened to her mother."

"Where are you going?"

"Remember, one of the victim's girlfriends told us about that new boyfriend?"

"Yeah, of course. What about him?"

"The other night, it was bothering me that we'd been forced to put it aside, and I pulled the case file out to keep in touch with it. I didn't want it to go too cold, and I started to check into this guy, Barry Eisner."

"And?"

"He could be the killer. The guy has a record, and he almost choked somebody to death in a bar fight."

"That's where you're going? To see him?"

I nodded.

"I know you were trying to keep me out of it, but you can tell me anything, Frank. We're more than partners."

"I trust you with my life, buddy, but you're a helluva lot younger than me, and I don't want to screw up your career with insubordination."

"And what happens if Eisner is the murderer? What are you going to tell the sheriff, then?"

"I'll work that out, if and when."

"We'll find a way to build a story. Don't worry."

"Thanks. Work your way through your part of the list. I'll talk to you later."

Chapter 32

I wound my way through a golf community known as Twin Eagles. Barry Eisner was a foreman for a roofing outfit that was putting a new roof on a home. I pulled up behind a truck with two men in it.

Spanish music was playing. Men on the roof were tossing tiles into a dumpster in the home's driveway. The guy behind the wheel looked like he could be Eisner. I knocked and stuck my badge against the window.

Cold air streamed out as he opened the window. "What, some neighbor pissed at the music?"

Eisner had a couple of days' worth of stubble but looked good with it. With the hassle of shaving and the price of razors, I wished I could get away with the look.

"No. I want to ask you a couple of questions."

"About what?"

"Jillian Evans."

He stiffened and opened the door. As he stepped out, he told his coworker he'd be right back.

Being thin was the only commonality between the men in Jillian Evans' life. Barry Eisner had a cowboy's good looks and the worn jeans to go with it. I pictured him with a red bandanna around his neck.

Crossing his arms, he leaned against the back of the truck. "What do you want?"

Eisner was as cocky as they came. "I understand you and Jillian Evans were in a relationship."

"Yeah, so?"

"Look, we can do this the easy way, or I can drag your ass downtown."

He shifted his weight but remained silent.

"When were you dating Jillian Evans?"

"Last time I saw her was about five weeks ago."

By using weeks as a measurement, was Eisner trying to make it look like it was longer than it was?

"How long were you in the relationship?"

"I don't know, a couple of months."

"How did you meet?"

He picked at a callous on his hand. "We had a job next door to her house. One day we started talking and we clicked."

No use beating him up on the time frame. I'd get the records from his employer.

"Was she seeing other men during that time?"

"It's a free country; she did what she wanted."

That was a yes. "Did that make you mad?"

He averted his eyes.

"You have anger issues, don't you?"

"What are you, some kind of shrink?"

"You were arrested twice for assaulting someone."

"Some guys got big mouths."

"A guy says something you don't like, and you go after him?"

"So, I got into a fight with a couple of guys. We were drunk; it was nothing."

"Nothing? You choke a guy until he goes unconscious and have to be pulled off him, and you call that nothing?"

"I said I was drunk."

"Were you drunk when you choked Jillian?"

"I had nothing to do with what happened to her."

"Where were you on the morning of March fifth? Specifically, the time between eight a.m. and ten a.m."

"I was working."

"Where?"

"I don't know."

"You don't remember where you were the day an ex-girlfriend was murdered?"

He shrugged. "We do a lot of jobs. You know how many roofs we put on?"

"You're going to need to tell me where you were, and who was with you the morning Ms. Evans was strangled."

He took a step away from the truck. "Where do you think you're going?"

"I got a job log in the truck."

Eisner grabbed a clipboard and flipped a page over. "You said March fifth, right?"

Like he forgot. "You know the date."

"We were working in Briarwood, by Naples Airport, that day."

It wasn't more than a fifteen-minute drive from the Evans house. "You were there all day?"

I tried to see the clipboard, but he turned it away.

"Yeah, we're doing a shitload of houses in there. They should have replaced most of them after the hurricane."

"Who was with you?"

"A lot of guys. I have three crews I'm responsible for. Each one of them is five men."

"You oversee the jobs they're doing?"

"Yeah, I make sure they're protecting the home and that they're working safely."

The men were walking on the roof without a tether, tossing piles of heavy tiles around. It was anything but safe.

"You go from site to site?"

"You gotta stay on top of these guys, otherwise they'll be taking breaks left and right."

"Doing what they do is a tough way to make a living."

"Tell me about it. I did it for two years. It sucked the life out of me."

"Let me ask you. Who do you think killed Jillian?"

"The ex-husband, George."

"What makes you say that?"

"He couldn't get enough of her. He'd call her all the time and bother her. He was a pain in the ass. I mean, she divorced the clown, but he didn't get the message."

Eisner was a rowdy troublemaker who'd choked a man until he blacked out. Still, he was a long shot in the suspect department. I finished up with him and called Derrick.

"How did it go with Eisner?"

"We need to check into his alibi. He claimed to be working in Briarwood the morning of the murder. Do you know if it's a gated community?"

"No. I've never been there."

"We need to find out if it is and if they have cameras. Then I'll check with Eisner's employer, see if they can verify where he was supposed to be working that day."

"Did he say anything else?"

"He offered George Evans as the murderer. Said that Evans wouldn't leave her alone."

"You think he is deflecting?"

"We'll find out. How are you doing with the DMV list?"

"On number thirty-four. Nothing yet."

"Keep working it. When I get back, I'll help you after checking Eisner's alibi."

***

Pushing through the parking lot door into the station, I felt reinvigorated. The Evans case was not quite live, but I'd moved it forward. If I had to work it covertly until the robbery gang was arrested, I would.

The line had been crossed already, and Derrick knew as well. I was comfortable with my decision. That is, until I thought about what Mary Ann would say about it.

She played by the rules and would probably be pissed at me, throwing the "ruining your career card" at me. She was right, but only to a certain point. Besides my family, bringing someone to justice for committing a homicide was what made me tick.

Derrick leapt up when I entered the office.

"We got him." He swung his monitor around. "Look at these."

Two pictures of a man were side by side. The left image was the one we took off the Winn-Dixie footage, and the second photo was from a driver's license. They were one and the same man.

"It's him all right." His name was Ernesto Mondolez, a thirty-four-year-old Hispanic.

"I'm surprised he lives in Naples. I was sure these guys were out of Lehigh Acres."

"We're not in the zip code business. You have to be open-minded. Some places may be safer than others, but don't fool yourself. Shit can and does happen everywhere."

"I know, just saying. We going to bring him in?"

"Eventually. Right now, I'd like to watch him for a bit. See if we can get more than him driving the mystery woman to the grocery store."

"But she's the one who pawned the watch."

"Yep, but he wasn't there. If he sticks to the story that he just brought her to get milk, we're screwed."

Chapter 33

Mondolez lived in an apartment complex that backed up to Goodlette-Frank Road, a series of burgundy buildings with zero architectural interest. Built in a U formation, there were over thirty identical square boxes surrounding a grassy area with a pool and tennis court.

We were watching the building at the bottom of the U that Mondolez's license said he lived in. He was probably home, as his gray Honda Pilot was diagonally parked across from it.

As a mother pushing a stroller came into view, the frustration of waiting hit me. What the hell was I doing sitting in a car on a stakeout like a rookie? I managed resources like someone living off the grid. It was the only way to run a homicide department with one other detective in a county with over three hundred thousand people.

The demographics of Collier County played a role in our small force. The annual per capita murder rates in the nation were just over five for every hundred thousand people. Ours was a fraction of that. If we didn't have such a low rate, we'd be dealing with twenty corpses a year instead of the dozen during the entire time I'd been here.

Numbers can be deceiving though. As hard as I tried, the annual number of killings were creeping up. As a father and a detective, it was a worrisome trend that I'd promised to reverse. Despite my vow, I had allowed my partner and me to waste precious time hoping we'd solve a robbery case, so we could go back to the Evans case. I had to do something.

"This is crazy. I'm calling Chester. Let him send someone to sit here. When and if they see something, they'll call us. Until then, we'll get back on Eisner's tail."

"What do you think he'll say?"

"I don't care what he says. This is a complete waste of manpower. We have a daughter whose mother was murdered. It's on us to bring the kid a measure of justice."

I punched the speed-dial button for the sheriff. "Miriam, it's Detective Luca. Is the sheriff available?"

Derrick said, "That's Mondolez. He's on the move."

"Forget it. I'll call you back."

Mondolez was lighting a cigarette. I said, "I'm not going to watch this guy like a rookie. Come on, let's see what we can shake out of him."

It was a risky move, but sitting on my hands wasn't in my playbook. Besides, we could probably search his car. We started toward Mondolez. When he saw us, he tossed the cigarette and ran west, cutting through a backyard onto the next street. Derrick was closing in on him, and I was struggling, falling behind.

Sucking air, I watched Mondolez grab the top of a white fence, with my partner just steps behind. As the suspect crested the barrier, Derrick grabbed his legs and pulled him to the ground.

I got there as he slapped cuffs on him. Hands on knees, I said, "Good work. You were like lightning."

"No problem."

Not for him it wasn't. Was the extra padding I was carrying what held me back?

I called for assistance. Pulling Mondolez to his feet, Derrick said, "Why'd you run?"

The suspect shrugged.

I said, "Search him."

Derrick patted him down and emptied his pockets. He held up a wad of cash. "Where'd you get this?"

"Playing cards."

I said, "Walk him back. Let's check out the car."

We didn't have anything except that he ran and circumstantial connections, but there was case history that allowed us to search a car without a warrant. Plus, we had the keys, making it easy.

Gloves on, I opened the driver's door and turned my head away. The smell of stale cigarettes roasting under the sun was disgusting. The glove compartment had a roach clip and a joint in a baggie. I got on my knees and looked under the seat. I didn't know what I was expecting, but it wasn't the pair of quarters I found.

A patrol car arrived, and we handed Mondolez off. "Pop the trunk."

Derrick put the key in and opened the lid. A furniture blanket was covering the top of a cardboard box. I pulled the blanket off and smiled at the pile of Popeye masks.

We had the string. All we had to do was tug it and unravel the gang that prevented me from hunting down Jillian Evans' murderer.

Chapter 34

Just before stepping into the office, my pee alarm went off. Again. I had been diligently following my doctor's orders by taking leaks every couple of hours. This was the first time I'd ignored the reminder in a month.

Derrick was writing on the whiteboard when I came in. I needed to go to the bathroom.

"Briarwood is gated. They have three entrances, two on Radio and another on Livingston."

"Cameras?"

"Yep."

"What about Eisner's alibi?"

"Waiting on a callback from the manager."

"I'm gonna take a piss. Then we'll go see Wild."

Two burglary detectives were washing up. I said hello and slipped into a stall. When I came back to work after losing my bladder, the guys would bust my balls because I had to sit like a woman to urinate. Now, no one said a word. Maybe political correctness had a good side to it.

I was looking forward to pressing Wild on his alibi. It was a mystery why people lied to the police so often. Was it the TV shows that made cops look like fools? I know it sold tickets, but movies about corrupt or incompetent cops burned me up.

We were protectors. The same people taking shots at us would be the first to call us when they needed help. Over my career, I'd worked with scores of men and women. Sure, there were a couple of lazy officers but rarely a corrupt one. It was perception over reality.

I tickled my abdomen to get a flow going, and my stomach growled. What was I going to have for lunch? I remembered Mary Ann had packed me something healthy to eat. Instead of a burger, I'd be chomping on carrots and hummus. Not entirely appetizing, but I was saving eight bucks a day and needed to drop weight.

We still hadn't gotten completely over the Jimena thing. It was stupid. If she'd just say she made a mistake hiring her without telling me, we could move on. I didn't like the tension between us, but I was worried that if I caved on something I felt was so fundamental, we might never recover.

How could she think it was okay to do that? We were not only talking about a caretaker for our daughter, but it made a mockery of the partnership between us.

Looking at my reflection, I vowed that if she didn't apologize, I'd have to find a way to talk it over without losing it, some way to heat up the chill in the air.

Derrick was cracking his knuckles when I walked back in. "Just got a call back from the roofing company."

"And?"

"Eisner was in Briarwood that day, but guess where else Eisner had been?"

"You know I don't like when you give me that guessing crap."

"Sorry. He was at Manor Care Health. The place right behind the Evans house."

"Whoa. What exactly did they tell you?"

"Eisner was supervising three crews in Briarwood that day. But they had just finished a job at Manor Care, putting a roof on a rehab wing."

"How'd you find out about that?"

"I just figured to ask about Manor Care because when I drove over there, I saw a building with a new roof."

"Good thinking, Derrick. You're really using your head. I'm proud of you, man."

"Thanks. Do you want to confront him?"

"Not yet. Get over to Briarwood, and get the video. We don't need much. Say from eight a.m. to eleven. See if we can find him leaving and coming back."

"Okay."

"Don't forget to verify what truck Eisner had that day. We don't know what kind of fleet they have."

"You got it."

"Oh, and check to see if there was anybody else with him. Another manager or anything. He had someone in the truck with him that wasn't a laborer when I saw him the first time."

"I'm on it."

"I'll see you later. I'm gonna see Wild."

***

The confirmation that Brian Wild wasn't working at Tamiami Ford as he claimed was a crimson-colored flag. But the information that Derrick had gleaned from a coworker edged it toward Ferrari red. When combined with the real possibility a court would strip full custody from Wild, it turned scarlet.

The service manager at the car dealership was Bill Pearson. He told Derrick that Wild had lost his temper twice on the job. One of the times, Wild had even gotten into a fight with a coworker because the guy kept lowering the thermostat that controlled the parts department.

It was a common point of contention. Half the people thought their workplace was too cold, and the other half too warm. Though I could sympathize with being cold, becoming physical over the temperature was a sign of instability.

Derrick was pushing to bring him in and interrogate him. I knew we needed a rounder picture of who Brian Wild was. If he really was a hothead, his neighbors would know about it.

Before heading out, I made a call.

"Jenny Robbins?"

"Yes, who is this?"

"Detective Luca. I wanted to see how you were doing."

"I'm fine."

"And your husband? Is he behaving himself?"

She hesitated. "Yes, everything is fine."

"Are you sure?"

"Yes, I'm positive. I've really got to go."

***

A cool-looking corporate jet was coming in for a landing as I drove by the airport. Its tarmac was lined with private planes. It was high season, and the wealthy were in town in full force.

The Ford dealer's parking lot was jammed. It debunked the perception of what Naples was. Everyone noticed the private jets and Bentleys, but the fact was, the majority of people in Naples were eating in restaurants that didn't have thirty-page wine lists.

A salesman, about to give a couple a test drive, pointed me in the direction of the parts department. Going through the crowded showroom, I had to wave off two sales associates.

Having a cop show up at your workplace is always embarrassing, but after the bullshit Wild fed me, I was less than concerned about making a scene. I told a kid behind the counter who I was, and he went to get his boss.

Wild came out smiling. "Detective Luca. Good to see you again."

We clasped hands. His shake had lost its mojo. "Is there a place we can talk?"

"Come on back to my office."

Wild's space was more cubbyhole than office. It held a metal desk, black roller chair, and a credenza crammed with pictures of his daughter. When he closed the door, I took a deep breath to quell my claustrophobia.

"You didn't catch the guy who did it, did you?"

I took my Moleskine out. "No. Why did you lie to me?"

"What are you talking about?"

"You told me you were here, working, the morning that Jill was murdered."

"I'm sure I was."

"You want to reconsider that? Your manager said you came in around noon and that you had told him you had gone to the doctor."

"Oh, right, I must have screwed up the dates or something. You know, my memory isn't what it used to be."

I did know. Except my memory issues were from getting dosed with chemotherapy.

"So, you weren't here on the morning of March fifth?"

He faked a laugh. "Nah, I had to go to the doctor. My cholesterol is out of control. Nothing I do seems to work."

"What doctor did you go to?"

"Uh, Dr. Cristaldi. He's on Pine Ridge."

I jotted down the information.

"And you didn't remember that?"

"Between working and running Joyce to soccer, dance, music lessons, and who knows what, I get things mixed up every now and then."

He was doing everything alone. It wasn't easy being a single parent, and it could have been an honest mix-up. Besides, we had Eisner in focus.

Chapter 35

I rolled my chair over to Derrick's desk. "What truck did Eisner have?"

"White Ford. An F-150 with red lettering on it. Roof rack with ladders."

"Let's see if he left."

Derrick hit play, and we watched a stream of vehicles enter Briarwood through the Livingston Road entrance. Those without transponders stopped at the main gate before entering the community. At 8:09, three trucks laden with ladders came into view. The first truck was a white Ford pickup emblazoned with the name Murphy Roofing.

It was Eisner, and he was alone. He pulled up to the guardhouse, chatted for a second, and the gate lifted. The trucks followed Eisner into the community.

"Let's check the exit lanes."

Derrick switched thumb drives. "Where should I fast-forward to?"

"Probably no more than fifteen minutes."

The flow of cars out of Briarwood was low. We examined the vehicles until 10 a.m. but didn't see any Murphy Roofing trucks leave. Derrick swapped out the main entrance video for the footage of vehicles transiting the access road off Radio Road.

He fast-forwarded to 8:30, and we watched residents leave their community to do their errands. As the time stamp hit 8:42, a white truck came into view. I said, "Slow it down. That looks like Eisner."

"Yep, it's a Murphy truck."

We watched frame by frame. There was no doubt it had left and was carrying only the driver. It looked like Eisner.

"That's him, Derrick."

"Geez, another bullshit alibi."

"He avoided the main entrance."

"It's closer to the Evans house."

"All right. Put the arrival video in. Let's see when he came back and through what gate."

Derrick changed drives. "Bet you he uses Radio to sneak back in."

Sure enough, at 9:47 the white Ford drove up to the guardhouse. He stopped, and the gate lifted. We made sure the license plate matched.

"What do you want to do next, Frank?"

"None of the neighbors mentioned seeing a roofing truck by the Evans house."

"There's nowhere to park over there. You have to get in a driveway."

"Check with Murphy's Roofing. See if they had any other jobs at any houses within walking distance of the crime scene. He probably went to Manor Care. If Eisner killed Jillian, he had the perfect cover with a job right behind the house."

"It could have been him the neighbor and pool guy saw."

"We'll need to get them to look at pictures of Eisner. Maybe we'll get an ID."

"We can use a quick solve."

"If they confirm it's him, we're still a long way from pinning it on him. We need to confirm that he was at Manor Care and not at another job site."

"I'll get over there and grab the video they have."

"If we confirm he was there, then we'll see about asking the witnesses. We have to be careful. Eyewitnesses can be unreliable, especially if we start running photos of Eisner by them and he gets cleared."

Derrick grabbed his sports jacket and said, "Be back in a flash."

Time was the number one enemy of solving crimes. Memories fade, evidence deteriorates, and the sense of urgency wanes as the clock ticks. I opened my Moleskine, flipping to the Wild interview. The doctor he went to see was Dr. Cristaldi. It was worth a shot. I looked up his office number and called.

"Dr. Cristaldi's office."

"My name is Detective Luca. I'm with the sheriff's office. I need information on a patient of yours."

"I'm sorry, Mr. Luca, but we're unable to share patient data without a court order."

"Ma'am, I'm not looking for anything private. All I want to know is whether a patient had visited your office at a particular time."

"I'm surprised at you, Detective. You should know that we are unable to share that information with you."

"I'm just asking for a little help here. It's a homicide investigation, and we've got limited resources. Clearing this up would save us a boatload of time and enable us to spend our time catching the killer."

"I'd like to help you, but I can't."

"I understand; thank you for your time."

Keeping medical records private was something I agreed with. But whether you went to the doctor or not? What the hell was wrong with sharing that information with law enforcement?

Getting a subpoena for such basic information was a symptom of how screwed up the system was. Now I had to ask Wild for proof. Who knew if he would try and fabricate documentation to support a visit?

"Mr. Wild? This is Detective Luca."

"Uh, yes, this is Brian Wild."

"I'm going to need you to document your visit to Dr. Cristaldi."

"Document it?"

"Yes. Show me the paperwork. The receipt for a co-pay with a time stamp or credit card transaction would work."

"I paid the co-pay in cash. It was twenty bucks. Nobody gave me a receipt because the doctor probably pockets it."

"You have no proof you were there?"

"I don't know. I'm at work. I'll have to look when I get home."

"I'll expect a call in the morning."

***

"Come on in, Frank. You want something to drink?"

"No thank you, sir."

"I'm sorry I didn't thank you sooner for nailing the Popeye gang, but the Orlando conference had me tied up."

"No problem. I hope you enjoyed the meetings."

"There's value in meeting with sheriffs from across the nation, but it could be done in two days instead of three. But enough about that. I wanted you to know how grateful this department and county is. That gang could've crushed tourism to the area. As a small token of my appreciation, I'm adding a special parking place for employee of the year, and you've earned it with these arrests."

"Thank you, sir, but that's not necessary."

"Maintenance is already on it."

"Thank you, sir. I'm just glad we were able to shut them down, so I can get back to solving the Evans murder."

Chapter 36

I stared at the frozen frame of a truck emblazoned with Murphy Roofing. The white Ford was pulling into Manor Care Health's driveway the morning Jill Evans was strangled to death. Eisner's employer had confirmed that the roof replacement they were doing at Manor Care had been finished three weeks before the murder.

What was Eisner doing there? Checking other camera feeds, we spotted Eisner walking around the rear of the building toward a parking lot. The camera's view didn't extend past the first row of cars, but we knew the lot ended at the preserve leading to the Evans' house.

I rewound the video covering the rear of Manor Care. At the edge of the sidewalk that fronted the parking lot, three men dressed in scrubs were smoking. Eisner was only a handful of truck lengths away. They had to see him. Eyewitnesses could be problematic, but three of them would be compelling.

Eisner had arrived at 8:56 a.m. and worked his way to the back of the complex, where we lost sight of him. Where had he gone? Was it to the Evans' house? What other explanation could there be? He thought he was smart, but all killers do. They just didn't know I'd be in relentless pursuit.

There was nothing on camera showing him leaving, but there was another exit leading to Lely Palms Drive that he could've taken. It didn't matter much. We had him returning to Briarwood at 9:47 a.m.

Fifty-one minutes had elapsed. Allowing fifteen minutes to drive back to the job site, Eisner had over half an hour to sneak through the woods, get in the Evans' house, and kill her.

I didn't like Eisner one bit. Did he think he was smart enough to kill an ex-girlfriend and get away with it? That would clearly be premeditated. It could have spun out of control after he got to Jill's house.

However, the fact he sneaked off the job, using Manor as a midpoint before slipping through the preserve, proved a level of planning impossible for any defense attorney to explain away.

We had the neighbor and pool tech that had seen a man in the preserve that morning. If they could identify Eisner as that person, we'd be on our way to a solve. Still, we'd need more to close the case.

A DNA sample from Eisner would be the clincher in throwing his arrogant ass behind bars if it matched one found on the victim.

***

This was the second time I had to fight the traffic on Airport Pulling Road to talk to Brian Wild. If there was one thing I hated more than a liar, it was anyone who wasted my time.

People thought nothing about making others wait or squandering their time on useless endeavors, but God forbid they had to wait in a store to check out. Why was it their time was more valuable than mine? And what really drove me crazy were those who made a fuss over losing time were the ones who would waste their days watching TV or a host of other unproductive time sucks.

The Ford dealer was bustling. I blew right past an approaching saleswoman and headed to the parts department. Wild was behind the counter with a kid a few steps away. He spotted me and said to his coworker, "Give me a few minutes alone."

I leaned into Wild.

"Do you know lying to the police is obstruction of justice?"

That was half true. You had to know you were making a false statement about the commission of a crime. At this point, as far-fetched as it appeared, Wild could have mixed up the dates, proving he had a worse memory than I did.

The color drained from his face so fast he looked like a coloring book figure. "I, I didn't lie."

"You've wasted enough of my time. First, you said you were at work the morning that Jillian Evans was murdered. Then you said you went to the doctor."

"I did."

"But you never documented it. You promised to call me. My phone works fine, but I never heard it ring."

"I forgot. You don't know how busy it is raising a daughter and working full time."

I did know, but I had a wife to share the workload. Wild was doing it alone.

"I understand; however, if you don't provide a verifiable alibi, being busy is going to be the least of your problems."

"I'll call the doctor's office and tell them to give you whatever they want."

"All I need is the date and time you were there. I don't care about anything else."

"Okay."

"Get on the phone with them. Put it on speaker."

Wild called and asked that the information be given to me. The receptionist told him they'd need the request in writing and directed him to their website, where the consent could be downloaded.

Wild pulled down the form, executed it, and emailed it back. We called the doctor's office, and the woman told us they'd pull the file in the morning. As insurance, I took the form with me when I left.

Chapter 37

I slammed the phone down. "I am going to throw this bastard in jail!"

Derrick said, "Who you talking about?"

"Brian Wild. The frigging guy couldn't tell the truth if his life depended on it."

"What's he lying about now?"

"The doctor's office said he was there, but two days after Evans was killed."

Derrick jumped to his feet. "It's got to be him."

"Let's go see our number one suspect."

If I was buying a car, I wouldn't go to a dealership so many times in such a short span. Tamiami Ford wasn't busy at ten in the morning, and all the salespeople trained their eyes on us as we walked in. A torrent of whispering began as we headed toward the parts department.

Wild was behind the counter tapping on a keyboard. His eyes bounced between us.

"What's the matter?"

I said, "Let's go to your office."

With only two chairs, we silently agreed to stand. When Derrick closed the door, I had to focus on the task at hand to keep my claustrophobia at bay. I took a deep breath and said, "Either you come clean, or we're bringing you in on suspicion of murdering Jillian Evans. You weren't at the doctor's office, and unless you can prove beyond a reasonable doubt where you were, you're coming with us."

Derrick said, "You weren't at work or the doctor's. Where were you the morning of March fifth?"

Wild hung his head. "I was with a woman at the Flamingo Hotel. In Bonita Springs."

"What's her name?"

"Rosalta Morales."

I asked, "How did you pay for the room?"

He reached for his wallet. "Credit card. I got the receipt."

"Help me understand this. Why didn't you just tell me you were with a lady friend?"

"I don't know. I was embarrassed."

"Because you went to a hotel with a girlfriend?"

"She's not exactly a girlfriend."

Derrick said, "What is she, the wife of one of your buddies?"

"No. I'd never do something like that."

I said, "Enlighten me. Who is this woman, and what are her contact details?"

***

Derrick came into the office shaking his head. "No dice. Eisner wouldn't agree to come in for a lineup."

"I didn't think he would. I was hoping since the two of you were about the same age, you'd have a better shot."

"A cop is a cop to him."

"No DNA either?"

"He gave me the bullshit that we'd use it to frame him. What's with people? Do they really think we do that?"

"I'm not saying it doesn't happen, but certainly not as often as you see on TV."

"Most cop shows are total BS."

"The legal ones are worse. They make it seem like it's drama after drama instead of hours of boring testimony and eons for a judge to decide whether to allow something."

"Shows with jurors nodding out wouldn't last too long."

"No doubt. Look, even though it's a long shot, I spoke with the DA about a photo lineup."

"Just headshots?"

"That was his preference, but I told him what the witnesses saw, and he agreed we could use full body shots."

"We don't have any of Eisner."

"Gianelli is on his way back now. Said he grabbed a couple of him."

"Good. Anything else?"

"The DA wants it to be sequential and recommended we use six instead of five fillers. I asked about conducting a second one sticking George Evans in it instead of Eisner, but he said a defense attorney would have a field day with it, claiming we were fishing."

"Let me run down the pool tech and landscaper. I'll get 'em in as fast as possible."

After Derrick left, I stared at the whiteboard. Right under a picture of Jillian Evans were photos of the men in her life. It felt like we'd know soon about her first husband, Brian Wild. He lied, but though it made me uneasy, I was hoping it wasn't him. Killing your ex to prevent her from taking custody would blow up everything I believed about parenthood. If it were true, even the most cynical New Yorker would have nothing over me in the skepticism department.

Then we had Eisner, the Marlboro man, who had been dumped by Jillian. He'd choked a man in a bar and lied about his whereabouts the morning Jillian was killed. The thing that didn't fit was the time element. There seemed to be too much distance between their breakup and the strangulation.

I didn't need a lesson in the patience a deranged mind could exhibit, and there was always the possibility that the relationship had restarted, like Jillian had done with George Evans. Hoping the lineup would clear things up, I moved to George Evans. As a former husband and rekindled lover, he was the classic suspect.

We had learned a lot about him, none of it good. His story about what he did the morning he found his ex-wife dead didn't quite fit. He didn't like—no man would—that his former was living with another man, especially a younger and more affluent one. I looked at the picture of Jafar Kapur.

The techie didn't look like a suspect. He was into life extension. Who wasn't? But had that kept us from drilling down on him? His relationship with Jillian was coming to an end, but he was successful, and in Naples there was no shortage of females, or males, for that matter, looking to attach themselves to money.

I pulled out Jafar's profile. It was as thin as he was. We needed to check with ex-girlfriends, neighbors, and coworkers. Either he's a suspect or he's not. Looking at the photo of him stapled in the folder, I remembered I needed to assemble pictures of men that I could use for the lineup.

Chapter 38

Derrick came into the office. "The pool tech is going to be here in an hour. But guess what?"

Here we go again. "What's that?"

"Wild was telling the truth this time."

"You tracked down the hooker?"

"Yeah, Rosalta was plying her trade at the Flamingo. Said Wild was a regular and would come to see her every ten days to two weeks."

"It's unbelievable. I felt bad for him when he said he went to her because a girlfriend would complicate things for his daughter."

"I don't know about that. I also saw the motel's video of him checking in. There's no doubt he was there. The Flamingo's manager said Wild was there a lot, always in the morning."

"He wasted a ton of our time. Call him, and tell him he's off the hook, but remind him about coming clean if something like this comes up again."

As Derrick spoke with Wild, I checked in with Mary Ann to make sure she was leaving at twelve. I didn't want Jessie to stay with anyone longer than a couple of hours. Though Jimena was the ice queen when it came to me, she and Jessie had bonded.

That was a good thing, but I didn't want the relationship to get too strong. Mary Ann told me she was leaving at one. I said I'd see her tonight and hung up.

Derrick said, "You're not going to believe it."

"What do you mean?"

"Wild, the story keeps getting better."

"And?"

"He got the clap from her. That's the reason he went to the doctor."

"Geez, that's disgusting."

"That's what you get for screwing around with a hooker."

The entire episode unsettled me. I was pissed at Wild for lying, but the circumstances were complicated. Here was a guy whose wife had gotten so depressed she lost custody of their daughter. I didn't know much about Wild, but I knew raising a child on your own was tougher than it had to be, and I admired those able to do it well.

Was Wild a weirdo because he went to a prostitute? Or was he a guy who didn't think he had enough time to nurture a relationship? Maybe the simple explanation was best: he was a father concerned that bringing a woman into his daughter's world would upset things, so he went elsewhere to satisfy his physical needs.

People rationalized their behavior in perplexing ways. With my experience in law enforcement, that reality wasn't a revelation. However, the context for Wild was too close to home. I believed I knew myself, but seeing this made me question how I would have acted.

I didn't think I could ever do something like that. But could I? Wild made a decision not to pursue a girlfriend because he was afraid he'd upset the relationship with his daughter. Then, he made a bad call going to a hooker for sex. One thing led to another.

A queasy feeling bubbled in my gut. I realized my desire to protect Jessie could easily cloud my decision-making process. I would have to be vigilant or risk screwing my life up.

***

The administrator of the lineup was a patrol sergeant who signed an affidavit that he knew nothing about the case. There was a bunch of protocol that needed to be covered before we could proceed. It was necessary if it was to be admitted into a courtroom as evidence, but it made me antsy.

I watched a live feed of the proceedings. The pool technician, Michael Borsky, was surfer boy relaxed. The sergeant, who was all business, asked, "Were you pressured to come here today?"

"No. They asked me, and I said sure. I mean, I gotta help catch this dude."

"Now, you should not feel compelled to identify anyone today. I don't know if the suspect is even in the photos you will see today, and neither do you. The investigation into this crime will continue whether or not you identify someone. Is that understood?"

"Yeah, the guy I saw in the back may be in one of the pictures or not."

"Are you ready to begin?"

"Sure."

"I'm going to show you seven photos. They're not in any particular order, and as I stated, may not contain a possible suspect."

"Okay."

"You can take as much time as you like with each picture. When you're ready to move on, let me know."

Borsky nodded.

"Here's the first one."

"No, it's not this guy."

The sergeant laid the second photo on the table. It was Eisner.

Borsky leaned over the photo before picking it up. It was making a connection with him. He shrugged, handed it back and looked at the next image. He quickly dismissed it and went through the other four.

"Would you like to see any of them again?"

"No. I don't think he was in there. If he was, I didn't recognize him."

I wanted to burst into the room. The only picture he picked up was the one of Eisner. He even gave a shrug like he was uncertain. Why didn't he want to see the picture again?

"Okay, let's take a ten-minute break before we go to the second series of photos. The restroom is down the hall on the right."

I was also going to use the pause to take a leak and headed to a bathroom in the opposite direction. I slipped into a stall trying to make sense of what I'd witnessed. It felt meaningless, like a waste of time.

It was difficult for me to resist the urge to go right out and haul Eisner in. I didn't need the confirmation from the pool tech. Eisner lied about his alibi. We had him a couple of football fields away on the morning of the killing. Why the hell had I thought it was such a good idea to do the lineup?

As a trickle of pee ebbed, I rehashed the episode. Why did everything have to be so difficult? Why couldn't Borsky pin the photo of Eisner as the man he saw in the preserve area?

I finished relieving myself and pulling up my pants, noticed the scar on my abdomen. It reminded me that nothing was easy. I never planned to get sick after moving to paradise. I wanted the doctors to confirm it wasn't cancer, just an infection that reddened my urine.

Washing up, I realized that what I wanted from the lineup was confirmation Eisner was the killer. I didn't want pushback. My confirmation bias needed stroking. That was dangerous ground for anyone, but especially for a homicide detective.

I watched the second lineup, wondering if the pool tech was intentionally screwing with my head. After passing quickly over the first four photos, he held the picture of George Evans with both hands. He stared at, turning it over as if expecting to find a note.

He tapped the edge of the picture on the desk and said, "Next."

It was impossible to predict what was going through this guy's mind. What were the odds of him giving extra attention to both suspects? Was it a crazy coincidence? Did a connection exist between George Evans and Barry Eisner? We knew Evans was there, but if he could be placed running through the backyard, we'd have something.

Even though we still had to see if the landscaper could identify the man he saw arguing with Jillian Evans, I knew what I had to do next.

Chapter 39

Using their own video feed, it didn't take Manor Care's administrator long to identify the smokers the morning of the murder. All three were Haitian males working as aides.

It was a tough but critical job that fell to recent arrivals to carry out. How well it was done was ground zero in determining the level of care a patient received.

The mother of the first man must have been clairvoyant. As soon as he stepped into the office, the room brightened. Luminous Bazin had a wide smile and a firm handshake. I couldn't help wondering if his name had predetermined his disposition.

"Have a seat. I have a couple of questions about someone you may have seen the morning of March fifth."

He had a heavy, French-influenced accent. "If I can help, no problem."

"Here's a picture of you and your friends smoking that morning."

"See, we go every time to take the break together."

I exchanged the picture for one of Barry Eisner. "Do you know this man?"

He nodded. "I think so."

"Can you be certain that you saw him the morning of March fifth?"

He squinted. "I don't know, maybe. I don't want to make trouble for him if I don't know."

"I understand. We have video of him on the security cameras."

"He do something bad?"

"We're trying to determine that. The morning in question, you were out back smoking with your friends, and this man, he would have walked to your left toward the back of the parking lot. Do you remember that?"

He shook his head. "No, sorry."

There was no use pushing. He seemed genuine. I thanked him and asked the second man to come in.

Paul Sasse also had a broad smile, one that contained as much gold as a small jewelry store. He was another man with a happy outlook. Was it escaping the poverty of Haiti that made them grateful?

"Mr. Sasse, I understand you and your friends take your smoking breaks together."

In a light accent. "Yes, yes. We do."

"On the morning of March fifth, just before ten a.m., you were out back having a cigarette. Do you remember?"

"Not exactly. But each morning I work, we go on break."

"Just to refresh your memory, here is a picture we took from the video camera of you and your friends that morning."

He smiled and nodded. "Yes, that is us."

"That morning a man walked to your left, from the building toward the back of the parking lot. Do you remember that?"

"What man?"

I held out the picture of Eisner. "This man."

"Oh, he the Romeo man."

"What do you mean by that?"

"He like to play with the girls."

"You mean flirting?"

"Yes."

"When did he do this?"

"I don't know. But I see him, two times, try, you know, make the dates."

"Did you see him that morning?"

"I don't remember, maybe."

I moved on to the next man, who was older. He was guarded, and I learned nothing from him. It was yet another frustrating waste of time. I spent an hour and a half canvassing workers and patients with rear-window views. I was looking for someone to confirm they'd seen Eisner emerge from the preserve, but apparently, I was looking for a ghost.

I knew I had to do the work and was willing to do it, but couldn't I catch a damn break once in a while?

***

There was no way I could miss another dinner. I wanted to catch Eisner at home anyway, so my plan was to play with Jessie, eat, then step out to see Eisner.

I jumped out of the car, hit the garage door button and jogged down the hallway. The smell of garlic and onions was in the air.

"Daddy's home. Where's my girl? Where's Jessie?"

My face hurt from smiling as she toddled her way toward me. "Da, da, home."

I scooped her up and got a cheek full of something sticky. "Where's Mommy?"

"Cocina."

Every day she was learning new words. But I wasn't a fan of her learning Spanish before she could speak English. That was another thing about Jimena. Just when I started to get used to her, this whole Spanish thing started.

I put Jessie on my shoulders and went into the kitchen, where Mary Ann was stirring a pan brimming with broccoli and cauliflower.

"Look how tall Jessie is. She's bigger than Mommy and Daddy."

"Wow. You're so tall, Jessica."

"How was your day?"

"Good, I got home at noon. Jimena had to leave early."

This nanny was running our lives. "Oh, everything okay?"

"Yes, she had something to do."

Oh, like the two of us? "What are you making?"

"Just some veggies, and I defrosted some Costco shrimp."

"Did you use that spice blend I picked up at Trader Joe's?"

"Yes, it smelled good."

"Any pasta?"

"Frank, you said you wanted to lose a little weight."

I sucked in my gut. "Come on, Jessie, let's go put the grill on."

"It's early yet."

"I need to step out after dinner and see someone."

She shook her head. "All right. Go ahead."

Mary Ann walked through a slider with a bowl of marinating shrimp. Jessie was holding a flower we'd picked.

"Mama, for you."

"Oh, it's beautiful. My favorite. Thank you, sweetie."

The shrimp gave off an aroma of paprika and turmeric as they grilled.

Jessie was in her high chair stuffing Cheerios in her mouth as Mary Ann chopped up a piece of shrimp for her.

I sliced open a tail. "Look at this, cooked to perfection by the master chef."

"Everybody gets lucky every now and then. Last week they were burnt, remember?"

"Someone must have slipped in and raised the temperature."

Mary Ann forked a small piece of shrimp. "Here you are, Jessica."

Jessie chewed away. "I think she likes it."

"Of course, her father made it."

"All right, Frank, time to change it up."

"Is it good, Jessie?"

"Si."

I lowered my voice. "This Spanish is getting out of hand."

"I bet it wouldn't annoy you if she were learning Italian. Would it?"

"Oh, come on. That's ridiculous, and you know it."

"I don't know why it bothers you. It's a good thing being bilingual."

"I know that. I just want her to learn English first."

"Maybe she would if you were around more."

"That's unfair. Things are crazy right now. It's a temporary situation."

Mary Ann forked another piece and fed it to Jessie. Her nonresponse was an answer in itself. I'd have to be careful, or it looked like I'd be in jeopardy of losing my right to complain about anything.

We finished dinner using Jessie as a shield. It wasn't the way I wanted this part of the night to go, but at least the shrimp seasoning hit the mark.

I hopped back in the Cherokee. It would have been nice to get another piece of evidence from somebody at Manor Care tying Eisner to going off the campus and returning. Unfortunately, it looked like my karma basket had a hole in it.

Turning onto Old 41, I took the snaky road across Bonita Beach Springs Road into Lee County. Eisner lived in a small single-family home on Abernathy Street. It was dangerously close to a tacos and wings joint I used to be too familiar with.

The house was another example of the shoemaker's kid needing shoes. Eisner's roof was missing a dozen tiles. The driveway was empty. It was a couple of minutes before 7:00 p.m.

After parking, I sent a text to Derrick to let him know where I was. I rang the bell. No answer, and no sign anyone was home. Gravel crunched underfoot as I walked along the side of the house to the back. There was nothing: no pool, lanai, or even a barbecue. Eisner hadn't adopted the Florida lifestyle.

Walking back to the front, I peeked in two windows. Not only was nobody home, there was hardly any furniture in the main room. It would be hard for anyone to spend time in this place.

I jumped back in the car and headed home. It was disappointing, but at least I'd get satisfaction out of surprising Mary Ann by coming home early.

Chapter 40

Derrick hung up the phone. "Murphy Roofing said Eisner didn't come in today."

"They say why?"

"No, he didn't call in."

"Uh-oh."

"Think he's onto us?"

"He could have gotten word from somebody at Manor that we were looking into him."

"If he disappeared because of it, he's our man."

"Call back his employer. See if he's done this before."

"Not showing up for work and not calling in?"

"Yeah, it's something many employers complain about."

"Basic decency is what it is. If it was my business, I'd fire anyone who didn't call in if they weren't in a hospital."

"I agree, but some businesses have to put up with it because they can't find workers. Especially with some less-than-desirable jobs like roofing."

"He's a supervisor."

"It's all about the culture. Give them a call. Then check the arrest records in Collier and Lee. For all we know he could be locked up."

Now we had two guys missing in action. The landscaper had vanished. It wasn't surprising since he was an illegal. It might take time, but we'd find him.

Rather than push the panic button on Eisner, we had to slow go it. He could've been sick, went to see a family member in trouble, or more likely, was shacked up with a new woman.

In the meantime, I'd use the next day or so to probe other suspects. It was either George or Jafar that I'd dig into. I decided to read through the notes of the interviews we'd conducted with Jillian's girlfriends. The physical abuse theme was what I wanted to focus on.

The hairstylist, Doris Parker, was where I started. She was one who mentioned that George had struck Jillian when they were married. She also claimed that Jafar had a temper, exploding when he found out that George was back in the picture. Something was missing from the interview.

Derrick interrupted my train of thought. "It's the second time Eisner didn't show up for work and hadn't called. The last time was about a year ago."

"A year? That doesn't exactly clear things up. Check the county jails."

I flipped through the case file. A yellow Post-it with my handwriting on posed a question: Pregnant - Who? That could be a motivating factor, and it was what I had failed to probe with Jillian's hairdresser friend.

"It's a good day at Parker Hair Designs. How can I help you?"

"Doris Parker?"

"Yes."

"This is Detective Luca. We spoke at your shop concerning Jillian Evans."

"Yes, of course. Are you looking to reduce some of the gray in your hair?"

I couldn't say I hadn't thought about it. "No, I'll let you know when I'm ready. I wanted to ask you about Jillian."

"What did you want to know?"

"Were you aware that Jillian was pregnant?"

"Yes."

"Did she tell you who the father was?"

"Yeah, she did."

"Who was it?"

"George, her ex-husband."

"Did she say how she felt about it?"

"She was confused. I mean, who wouldn't be, with her history."

"You mean the postpartum she suffered from?"

"Yeah, that plus everything that was going on with her. She wanted to start things fresh. Have Joyce with her and break away from the men in her life. Concentrate on being a mother, that's what she really wanted."

"Do you think she was going to carry the baby to full term, or was she thinking about abortion?"

"I think when she first found out, she was upset that it might screw things up with Joyce, and that was the last thing she wanted to do. Then, she seemed to get comfortable with it. Who knows, maybe in her mind she was thinking if things didn't work out with the custody battle, she'd have the new baby."

"What? Like some sort of consolation prize?"

"Excuse me?"

"Sorry, please forget that. I'm a little sensitive when it comes to kids and—"

"It's okay. I didn't mean to make her sound bad. She was a good person. I was just thinking maybe the way her mind worked after what happened . . ."

"I understand. Again, I'm sorry for what I said. Let me ask you this, did she tell George or Jafar that she was pregnant?"

"I don't know. All I know is that she was worried about how they'd take it."

"And you're sure that she wanted to end it with both men?"

"That's what she told me. Not once either."

Derrick was hovering over my desk. Was Eisner behind bars somewhere? I finished the call.

"Eisner was arrested?"

"No. There's no record of it."

"The way you were standing over me . . ."

"I heard you talking about who the father was. Who was it?"

I resisted the urge to ask him to guess. "George Evans."

"Interesting. That means he didn't kill her."

"Not especially. It could be she told him that she was going to abort the baby. Evans is a pro-lifer; it might have pushed him over the edge."

"That plus the fact she was going to leave him could have been the motive."

"For sure, having a baby is an emotional roller coaster."

"What about Jafar Kapur? If he found out she was pregnant by another man, he could've lost it."

"No doubt. But we don't even know if she informed one or both of them about it. She could've kept it quiet. It was early; she had time."

"True. Or she could've told just one of them."

"Or was killed before having the chance to tell the other one. If that was the scenario, it's likely she'd tell the father first. But we're getting too speculative at this point. First, we need to find out if she told them. Then we'll move to what the reaction was."

My email box chimed. It was from Joyce Wild. Just great. Eisner was the leading suspect, and he was nowhere to be found. I didn't want to read it. Maybe I could make like it went into my spam box. I hit open:

Hello Detective,

I wanted to ask about how finding out about my

mother is going.

I know you are busy, but you did promise to let me

know.

Please tell me. It's driving me crazy not knowing.

Thankfully, Joyce Wild.

Why did I respond to her in the first place? I wanted to tell her I couldn't comment, but I didn't want to dash this poor kid's hope.

The reply I ended up sending kept me doubting it was good enough. Telling her that we were making progress and that I hoped we would have good news soon seemed canned. Though it was brief, it had enough hot air in it to melt an igloo. I had the feeling that even though she was a kid, she'd know I was giving her a nonanswer.

Chapter 41

George Evans was out in the field again, this time in Victoria Shores, a collection of condos and coach homes on Airport Pulling Road. Entering the community, I remembered taking Mary Ann here when we first started dating. During Christmas, a number of the residents go overboard with lights.

One Cool Zone truck was in the driveway and another by the curb. A tech was spraying water on the compressor. I approached, asking, "Is George Evans here with you?"

"Yeah, he's inside wrapping it up with the customer."

"What are you doing?"

"Just cleaning the outside. These landscapers spray their shit on everything, and pesticides are corrosive."

"Wow. Say, how long you been working with George?"

"Why you asking that?"

"Just shootin' the shit. Me and George go back a while."

"Less than a year."

"He has some temper, right?"

"Guess so."

I wanted to explore it, but Evans was heading my way. He was holding a clipboard and slowed when he saw me. I met him halfway.

"I have a couple of questions for you."

"Now? I'm working."

"Yep, now."

He told his coworker he'd meet him at the next job.

"I thought you were the service manager."

"I am. We got slammed with service calls today, and replacing a coil is a two-person job."

"They don't make the units to last these days, do they?"

"Most of them are garbage. They'll never last more than ten years. Most of the midrange ones crap out around seven."

"That's crazy."

"It is, but it makes this business what it is."

"Did you know that Jillian was pregnant?"

"Pregnant? With a baby?"

"There's no other kind. Were you aware of that?"

"No. Who was the father?"

"I was hoping you'd know."

"How would I know?"

"You said the two of you were getting back together."

"We were."

"I would suppose that included sexual relations."

His pasty face reddened. It was hot, but he'd rubbed his neck. A classic body language signal that he was uncomfortable.

"It did."

"You're telling me you were having sex with your ex-wife, who became pregnant, and she never told you?"

His jaw tightened. "Maybe it wasn't mine."

"Who's would it be, then?"

Evans hands were fisted. "Why don't you ask that fucking Indian?"

"Jafar Kapur?"

"Who the fuck else?"

"I don't want to upset you further, but it's important. Do you think your ex-wife was having sexual relations with another man who could have been the father?"

His face was redder than his lips. "Do you think she would have told me that?"

"I not asking if she told you. I'm suggesting that since you knew her so well, you'd have a feeling. We know when something's not right. So, tell me what you sensed was going on."

"She was living with him. Any moron would know what was going on."

"When you restarted your relationship, I'm sure you didn't want her to date other men. Right?"

"Of course."

"Did you tell her not to?"

He sighed. "I told her it was me or nobody else. I didn't want to share her."

"And did that persuade her to end any relationships?"

"No."

"How did that make you feel?"

"How the fuck do you think being made a fool of feels?"

It had to be a blow to anyone, male or female, if their partner was playing around on them.

"You have no idea who the father was?"

"No, she never told me she was pregnant."

"According to one of her girlfriends, Jillian confided in her that you were the father."

"Me? Oh my God. I can't believe it. Are you sure?"

"That is what she told me."

"I can't believe this is happening. I can't talk about this. I'm too upset."

Watching Evans climb into his truck, I wondered what it was that he couldn't believe. Was it that someone had killed his wife and baby or that he had killed his own child? Whether his reaction was orchestrated or real was tough to decipher.

***

As soon as I walked back in the office, I asked Derrick, "Any word on Eisner?"

"Nothing. I even took a ride by his place just in case he was there, but no luck."

"If he doesn't show up by tomorrow, we may have to consider him on the run."

"That would make it likely he killed Jillian."

"Maybe, or he's running from something else. Eisner isn't a choirboy."

"For sure."

"I'd like you to go down to the landscape company where the illegal saw Jillian arguing with someone. Find his friend Rigoberto Gomez and tell him if his buddy doesn't surface and cooperate, we'll sic immigration on him."

"That should work."

"Maybe, but it could also drive him out of the state."

"I'm on it. What ever happened with Evans?"

"He claimed not to know that she was pregnant or that it was his."

"You believe him?"

"He said he was so upset that he couldn't talk about it. When he walked away, I didn't try to stop him."

"It doesn't mean he didn't do it. He could be upset to know he killed his own kid."

"Exactly what I thought. We know Jillian had a tough time deciding what man to stick with. What if she were going back with Jafar or told Evans that even though she was pregnant that she no longer wanted to be with him. Her friend Doris Parker said she was done with both men."

"The question is, what about the baby? Was she going to abort it? Maybe that's why she never said anything to Evans, or whoever the father was."

"George Evans was against abortion. Maybe he flipped out when she told him."

"But then he'd be killing the baby he didn't want aborted."

"I know, but if he went into a rage, he'd lose the ability to reason."

"If we could find out that George knew about the pregnancy, that would expose his shock at the news as phony and open a new line."

"Why don't you dig around some while we wait to see if and when Eisner shows. I'm going to see how Jafar reacts to this."

Chapter 42

Country music was playing again when I walked into Xtended Living. Trying to identify if it was Blake Shelton singing, I noticed about half the desks were empty. Was this another tech company who promised big and was flaming out?

Everybody knew money problems were stressful. I'd put my share of people in prison who'd made enormous mistakes under financial pressure, people who would normally not commit a crime if not for the clouded judgment a failing business or job loss brought. Was Jafar Kapur another example?

Jafar came of his office holding an armful of plastic bottles. He saw me, nodded, and set the containers on a colleague's desk. His smile was bright, but his demeanor told me he wasn't happy to see me.

"Detective, did you come by to sign up for DNA profiling of your telomeres?"

"I already forgot what they were."

"They're DNA segments at the end of our chromosomes. The key is how long they are. Short ones have a much higher mortality rate. We're confident that keeping them long, so they can continue to allow cells to divide, is the key to longevity."

"It sounds fascinating. I hope you figure it out, and fast."

"We will. There's no doubt in my mind. Right now, we know that you can keep your telomeres on the longer side by reducing stress and exercising regularly. Of course, nutrition plays a role as well."

I sucked my gut in, wondering if Mary Ann had talked to this guy. "Reducing stress is tough when you're a homicide detective."

"Have you tried meditation?"

No, and I had no plans to. "I've been thinking about it."

"Try it. People have been doing it for centuries."

Yeah? How come they were dying in middle age if it was so good for you? "I will. Can we talk privately?"

"Sure, come on back to my office."

The Google glasses were still on his desk.

"It's seems quiet around here today."

"A lot of people went to a tech conference."

"Got it."

He saw me looking at the Google glasses.

"You seem interested in the glasses."

"I guess I am. I told my wife about them. It just seems kind of hard to believe we'll be walking around wearing things like that."

"Oh, it's coming. In fact, the next generation pair is being shipped to me as we speak."

"Wow. A lot of improvements, I'd imagine."

"Indeed. Can't wait to see what they've done with them. The old ones are dinosaurs, from what I've read. You're more than welcome to take them. I'm just going to toss them anyway."

"Oh, I couldn't."

"Why not? I'm going to throw them out, so take them. You could show them to your wife."

"I don't even know how to use them."

He picked up the glasses and put them on. "It's super easy. You wear them like this, and in the upper right-hand corner is the viewing panel. Of course, you'll need to register them and have an internet connection, but the instructions are in here."

He reached into a drawer, pulled out a case, and placed the glasses in them. "Here, take them, or they're going into the trash."

"Thanks. My wife is going to get a kick out of them."

"No problem."

"Thanks again. Look, I wanted to ask you a couple of questions about Jillian."

"Still can't believe she's gone."

"Were you aware that she was pregnant?"

"Jill? Pregnant? No, I had no idea."

"Would you happen to know who the father may have been?"

"Well, it wasn't me, if that's why you're asking."

"You're certain?"

"We were having some issues. You know, relationship things. I was working too much, she said, and it turned her off. So, we hadn't been, you know, having any intercourse. Besides, when we did, she wanted me to use protection."

"I understand. Tell me about the problems the two of you were having."

"It was nothing really. Just normal things. Like I said, she was upset about how much time I put in here. She said I cared more about Xtended Living, but as much as this mission means to me, Jill was the center of my world."

"Were the two of you about to break up?"

"No, things were actually improving."

"A friend of Jillian's told me that Jillian was going to move on, ending her relationships with George Evans and with you."

"Look, I don't see how speculating about this is helpful. Jill is unfortunately gone."

"Would it surprise you to learn that George Evans was the father of the baby she was carrying?"

He jumped up. "Look, are you trying to upset me? I'm a busy man, and I can't waste time with your line of questioning."

It was a hot button for him. There was a rivalry with George Evans, but there always were when two men vied for the same woman. Still, it felt like an overreaction.

***

Derrick was tapping away at his keyboard when I came back in. Hanging my jacket up, I asked, "Any word on Eisner?"

"Nope. Still missing in action."

"Did you get anything on Evans?"

"No. This guy is a loner. Anybody who knew him says they didn't really know him."

"It's a wild card, but did you try his first wife?"

"No, can't imagine him telling her."

"He'd have to tell someone."

"That's why I put a call into his brother. He lives in Wyoming."

"Wyoming? What—the whole family loners?"

"Could have been a crazy childhood."

"Look into that as well."

"All right. How'd it go with the techie?"

"He was touchy when I brought up his rival, Georgie boy."

"No love lost between those two."

"And how. I'm going to dig a little into his background. We don't know much about him."

"We never got his DNA either."

I didn't want to tell Derrick that I'd just forgotten to ask him for a sample. My plan was to ask for it before we started talking, like I had done with Evans. It was never a good idea to ask for anything voluntarily after you started questioning someone.

Chapter 43

It was time to head home. I was looking forward to some family time after an unproductive day. It felt as if we were sitting around waiting for Eisner to show up, which was the polar opposite of how I chased down killers.

You had to act aggressively. If you waited for things to come your way, you were going to be screwed nine times out of ten. Success only danced with those who were on the dance floor.

I'd gotten a terrible parking spot, in the direct sun. The Cherokee would be an oven. I opened the driver's door and circled to the passenger side to open it, enabling the strong breeze to blow out the heat. When I swung open the door, I saw it.

Sitting right next to *Mr. Olsen's Meat Pies*, a book I bought for Jessie, was the case holding the Google glasses. I swept the case off the seat and leaving both doors open, headed back into the station.

After logging the evidence, I skipped down the stairs to the forensics lab. We had Jafar Kapur's DNA and would soon know if it matched the second specimen on Jillian Evans' body.

When I jumped back in the Cherokee, not only had the heat disappeared, but so had my frustration. I had something working: a possible answer to the DNA puzzle to go along with a new book to read to Jessie.

***

Waiting for Jafar's DNA results to be processed, I decided to check into his background. He had emigrated to the United States in 2002, seventeen years ago, becoming a citizen when he turned eighteen. The time line was incredibly quick in light of the 2001 terror attack.

After the planes were flown into the World Trade Center by Islamic terrorists, the gates into the United States were slammed shut. How'd he get in? It didn't make sense. There had to be an explanation. I knew there was a program that allowed people with certain desirable skills to come here. It was clear Jafar had a combo of medical and technology skill sets that any country would welcome. From what I knew, they granted visas to those people.

But it didn't make sense; he was a kid, just thirteen years old at the time. Was he a child prodigy?

Searching Homeland Security's database, which wasn't even around when Kapur came to America, I discovered two things. It wasn't surprising to learn that Jafar had come to America with his mother, Chanda, and his sister, Aashi.

What I didn't expect to learn was they'd been granted asylum. I hunted in the State Department's database, hoping there'd be a clue. The entire process was restricted due to privacy laws, but you never knew when a bureaucrat would make a mistake. Unfortunately, I hit wall after wall and gave up.

What were the circumstances that allowed the Kapurs to be waved through while hundreds of thousands of people fleeing persecution from Islamic extremists were turned away?

I needed to find out more by talking with his mother and sister. Both of them lived in Edison, New Jersey, where a high concentration of Indian immigrants had settled. Outside of reporting a break-in of their apartment, there was no record in the law enforcement touch files for either of them.

After leaving messages on a landline and the sister's cell phone, I made another call.

"Murphy's Roofing."

"I want to speak with the manager, please."

"He's out. Is this about a roof?"

"No, ma'am. I'm with the Collier County Sheriff's Office. I'm looking for Barry Eisner."

"He hasn't been in the last two days."

"Have you heard from him?"

"Not yet."

"Take my number down, and call me as soon as you see or hear from him."

"Is this about the murder of the Evans woman?"

"I can't say, ma'am."

"I'm just asking, 'cause it's kinda strange that we did a roof on the husband's house, like six months ago."

"You did?"

"Yep. I just had to look it up when it happened. I seen it in the paper, and sure enough, I remembered it."

"Do you know if Barry Eisner worked on that job?"

"He sure did."

I stumbled giving her my number and hung up. What the hell did this mean? Derrick had made some offhand comment about the possibility George Evans and Barry Eisner knew each other, but I had discounted it.

It was crazy, Evans and Eisner were romantic rivals. Did Evans know that his ex-wife was playing around with the guy who roofed his house? What were the chances that Evans had hired Eisner to kill his wife?

Why would Eisner agree to do it? Rearing its head again, the timeless motivators of money and love came to mind. The problem with money was that Evans didn't appear to have much. He had more than Eisner, but was it enough?

Eisner had been dumped by Jillian. Could his scorned pride have been the motivation for deadly revenge? The third possibility was a combination, where Eisner agreed to do it for a cheap price because he also wanted revenge; that made the most sense.

Eisner and Evans. It sounded like a law firm partnership. Could it have been a killing alliance instead?

Derrick came in holding two cups of coffee. "I guess it's official now. We got our marriage license."

One of the pleasures of life was the smell of coffee. "Congratulations. It's official, then."

"It didn't feel like anything. If I had to do it over again, I'd do it in reverse. Have the wedding in the church first, celebrate, and get the license from city hall."

I sipped the java. "That sounds like a good idea. We felt the same way about it. I don't know if the church will marry you without it though."

"What's going on?"

"You're not going to believe this—" I realized I was doing what he did to me. "Sorry, it looks like Eisner and George Evans knew each other."

"What? How?"

"Evans hired Murphy to put a roof on his place, and the supervisor was Eisner."

"I said that they knew each other, just kidding around. You think there's any chance they conspired to murder Jillian?"

"I don't know what to think. But we have to find out if Evans knew that Eisner was seeing his wife."

"You think Evans told Eisner to take off?"

"I don't know, but if they're in this together, I'm betting we crack Evans easier than Eisner. Evans will give him up in a heartbeat, especially if we dangle a deal in front of him."

"It's getting interesting."

"Guess what else I learned?" Was it contagious?

"What?"

"The way Jafar came into the country seems weird. He came with his mother and sister under an asylum claim."

"Asylum?"

"It seems crazy, especially since it was after nine eleven, when they shut it down. Less than half the normal amount was allowed in then."

"Maybe there was a threat against the family or something."

"Could be. But his father stayed in India with a brother."

"A lot of cultures are used to splitting their families up."

"I couldn't imagine it, especially now that we have Jessie. It would be heartbreaking. I don't know how they do it."

"They may not have a choice."

"I don't know. You always have choices. You may not like them, but they're there."

The phone rang as Derrick said, "I can see if you send your kid to the States for an education or maybe they need medical care you can only get here."

I picked up the phone, had a brief conversation, and hung up.

"That was forensics. Listen to this."

Chapter 44

We had a match. The DNA we lifted from Jafar's Google glasses matched the second specimen found on Jillian's corpse.

It wasn't earth shattering. It was likely his, meaning the killer was either George Evans or Jafar Kapur, or that someone like Eisner or a burglar was exceedingly careful. Considering the circumstances, like the pocketbook and purse being free of fingerprints, left open the possibility an intruder was a professional.

I rolled it around as Derrick went to the bathroom. I'd encountered a lot of professional thieves in my career. They were cautious and did their best to avoid leaving evidence behind. The key to the theory was in the booty they went for.

The pros would choose targets that rewarded their preparation. They generally looked for big scores. What Jillian Evans had wasn't in that category. Unless there was something we were missing.

Could there have been something valuable that she had? Was it illicit drugs? She had worked in a doctor's office years ago. Maybe she was involved in a prescription drug pipeline. As Derrick came back in, an idea hit me.

"You know, there is the chance that whoever did it hit the wrong house."

"What do you mean?"

"Assuming it's an outsider who did it. Let's say they were going to rob something valuable. What it could be, I don't know. But they simply make a mistake and hit Jillian's house rather than a neighbor's."

"That's a stretch."

"I know, but we need to consider all possibilities."

"You're right. You want to check out the neighbors?"

"Exactly. Not all of them, and nothing crazy. Say the two houses on either side of her. Run them through the system. See if anyone with a record pops up."

"Should be easy enough."

"If there aren't any hits, I'd like you to go out there and conduct interviews."

Derrick nodded as he picked up a ringing phone. "Detective Dickson."

"Yes, he's right here. Hold on a minute."

"Frank, it's some woman called Aashi. Is that Jafar's sister?"

"Yep, that's her."

"Hello, this is Detective Luca. Thank you for returning my call."

"Is everything all right with Jafar?"

"Yes, he's fine."

"Oh, thank God. My mother was upset when she heard your message."

"I'm sorry. I wanted to ask about your asylum claim when you immigrated."

"Are you with immigration?"

"No. You have nothing to worry about. We're doing some background work on a case that may have crossed paths with yours. I can't say much, but it could involve an official who worked in immigration back then."

"Oh. What do you want to know?"

"It was kind of unusual to be granted asylum back in 2002, with all the craziness after the terror attacks. How did you qualify for it?"

"My father was a violent man. He abused all of us: my mother, my sister, and me. He threatened to kill us, but no one would listen. When he choked my sister to death, we took a train to Delhi, with nothing but the clothes on our backs, and went to the American embassy."

The tone in her voice made it clear she had dealt with the trauma and was clinical about it.

"He killed your sister?"

"Yes and got away with it. He made claims that she had dishonored the family, and they let it go. The culture in India, I am sad to say, doesn't value women."

"I, I'm so sorry to hear this. I understand why this was a legitimate claim. Just one more question, if you don't mind."

"If you wish."

"I understand your other brother stayed behind with your father."

"Yes, he was just like my father, another monster."

"I'm sorry to have brought this up. Thank you for your time."

I hung up and leaned my head back.

"What's the matter?"

"Man, was that a disturbing call."

"What did she say?"

"That Jafar's father choked their sister to death and got away with it."

"What the hell?"

"The animal was abusive toward his wife and daughters. According to her, they complained about him, but nothing happened due to the way women are viewed in India. When he killed the sister, they fled to the American embassy."

"Holy shit. How screwed up is that?"

"It's as sad as it gets. Bastard got away by saying the kid dishonored the family."

"What, are they in the frigging Stone Age over there?"

I exhaled. "I need to get out of here for a minute. She really shook me up. I'm going to sit on a bench at Loudermilk Park for my lunch break."

"Sure. You want me to come along?"

"No, I need to be by myself. Do me a favor; go to the landscape outfit and lean on that guy. Tell them we're going to have immigration turn the place upside down if they don't get me Espeza."

***

I snaked my way along Gulf Shore Boulevard, passing blocks of low-rise condos that had been built in the sixties and seventies. Steps from the beach, whoever owned the units had probably paid nothing for them. Now they needed major upgrading, but their location was priceless.

I grabbed a pair of hot dogs and some fries from the food truck. It was the antithesis of the health food I was supposed to be eating, but the way I felt, I needed comfort food. Perched on a bench with a zillion-dollar view, I tucked into a frank.

A mother with two girls in pink bathing suits were digging in the sand under the shade of an umbrella. The mother motioned to them, and they jumped up and down as if Minnie Mouse had appeared.

The mother showed her children juice boxes, and the girls held hands as they went to get their snack. If you looked up the word cute, there'd likely be a picture of these kids.

My heart tugged as I thought of my own daughter. Jessie and these girls were depending on me to help keep them safe. The realization I could only do so much scared me more than cancer.

At some point every woman had to defend themselves against manipulative men. I always thought that people like me were the frontline, but to be effective, everyone had a responsibility to protect themselves, to fight and resist becoming a victim.

Chapter 45

I read two books to Jessie before bed. She fell asleep twice, but I nudged her awake. After finishing *Green Eggs and Ham*, I took her to say good night to Mary Ann.

She was in her crib nodding off for five minutes before going out cold. I stood over her for ten minutes before dragging the rocking chair over. Jessie was the most beautiful thing I had ever seen. I studied her heaving chest as Mary Ann came back in, whispering, "Frank, are you okay?"

Instead of saying yes or no, I shrugged. I put the chair back and followed her into the family room.

"What's going on?"

"I don't know. All this crap is starting to get to me."

"What are you talking about?"

"Kids, girls, even some women, they're vulnerable. How are we ever gonna protect Jessie? It's impossible."

"What in the world is going on with you?"

I told her what I learned from Jafar's sister.

"Oh my God, that's horrible."

"Disgusting. I wanna take bastards like him, line 'em up and shoot 'em, one by one."

"I can't believe you can get away with that in India."

"It's not just India! It's happening all over the world. I can't just sit and watch this—"

"Take it easy, Frank. I know you're upset, and it's a tragedy, but worrying about how to fix something ten thousand miles away isn't going to help. You do what you can. That's all you can do."

"Who's going to protect these girls?"

"You're not responsible for the entire world."

"If anything happens to Jessie, I swear, I wouldn't be able to go on."

"Nothing is going to happen to her. She's going to be fine."

"It's nasty out there."

"After eighteen years on the street, you don't think I know that?"

"I know you know."

"You can't put Jessica in every victim's situation. You'll go crazy that way."

"I'm not doing that."

She took my hand. "Yes, you are, Frank. And it's not healthy. I remember when I was taking psych courses in college, and I felt like every ailment we learned about I could detect in others."

That had happened to me as well, but I didn't feel like acknowledging it. I shrugged. "It's not the same."

"All I'm trying to say is you can't do that to yourself; you'll end up paralyzed."

"I'm just worried about her, that's all."

"So am I, but we keep doing what we are doing, and make sure we not only talk the talk, but act like we should, and she'll be fine. You'll see."

"I hope you're right."

"I am. Let me put on the dress for Derrick's wedding. I picked it up from the seamstress. I want to make sure it looks all right."

Mary Ann was more confident than I was. I agreed with the walk the walk part. I'd seen too many people, friends included, who talked a good game with their kids. The problem was they failed in the execution of being a model for the behavior they espoused.

Far from perfect, that was one thing I couldn't permit myself to do.

***

I smelled the coffee Derrick had brought before I saw it on the corner of my desk.

"Morning, Frank."

"Morning. No donuts?"

"I have to fit into a tux with a thirty-inch waist."

"They have those things on the side to adjust it."

"I promised Lynn I'd keep an eye on my gut. When we met, I had a washboard. It's long gone now."

I never had one. Not that I wouldn't have liked six-pack abs when I was thirty. I just didn't want to put the work in to try and get them.

"Mary Ann is on me as well." I patted my belly. "She wants me to take better care of myself. I will, but I'm not eating kale like she does. You ever taste that crap?"

"Green cardboard."

"If they made donuts with kale, I wouldn't eat them."

"I don't know if you'd go that far."

"Ha-ha. Look, I want to dig into Jafar, see what we can get on him. We don't know much, and with his family history, you never know what will turn up."

"Why don't we start by talking to a couple of his exes?"

"Exactly. I'm going to miss you when you go on your honeymoon."

"I was hoping we would have wrapped this up by then."

"We have almost two weeks."

If Eisner was the killer, we could make it, but if he didn't show up soon, we'd have to hunt him down. If he was on the run, he could be anywhere, and he had a couple of days' head start on us.

As Derrick worked at piecing together a clearer picture of who Jafar Kapur was, I wasn't going to let Eisner get too far out of my grasp. He was another guy we didn't have enough intel on, and I was going to collect more.

"Murphy's Roofing."

"Hi, this is Detective Luca—"

"We haven't heard from him."

"Okay. I want to know who Barry Eisner worked with. Not the laborers, per se, but anyone he spent time with. Anyone he was friendly with."

"I don't know anything about the friend stuff, but Jorge was the assistant site manager for the jobs Barry ran."

"What is Jorge's last name?"

"Melendez."

"Where is he now?"

"With Barry out, Jorge is covering three jobs, one in Pelican Marsh and two over in Grey Oaks."

"Find out where he is, and tell him to stay there. Don't let him know I'm going to go see him. I'll hold on while you track him down."

Coming in the back entrance on Airport Pulling Road, I drove down the center of Pelican Marsh, almost reaching the main gate on Tamiami Trail. There were close to two thousand homes in the community, spread over more than two dozen neighborhoods.

There were all kinds of price points and homes, and I was headed to Egrets Walk, a collection of coach homes. Several roofs, in the midst of being replaced, came into view as soon as I turned into the neighborhood. It looked like four buildings were being worked on. The homes were a good twenty-five years old. It was time to replace the roofs before they failed.

I pulled behind a Murphy's truck that was parked behind a dumpster filled with roofing refuse. The engine was running, and a man behind the wheel was talking on the telephone. I knocked on the window and pressed my badge against it.

A man with maple syrup skin and tattoo sleeves covering both arms said, "I'll move the truck, no problem."

"Are you Jorge Melendez?"

He hesitated. "Yes. I didn't do nothing. I'm working the roofs."

"I have a couple of questions about a coworker, Barry Eisner."

"Oh. What do you want to know?"

"Do you know where he is?"

He shook his head. "No."

"Are you sure you have no idea where he might have gone?"

"I don't know. I wish he comes back. We got too many jobs, and the workers listen to him more than to me."

"Is he rough on them?"

He shrugged. "You have to be."

"Give me an example."

"When we have the breaks, nobody wants to go back up; it's too hot. So, Barry, he has to make them get up there. Sometimes he push them."

"He hits them?"

"No, just yelling, pushing them."

"How long have you known him?"

"We worked together at Advanced Roofing."

"When was that?"

"When I first got to Fort Myers, about three years ago."

"You socialize with him?"

"Just a couple of times."

"What can you tell me about him?"

"He liked to go fishing."

"What type of person was he? Was he violent? Who were his girlfriends? Who did he hang around with?"

"He was okay, to me. He's the one who got me to be assistant. So, I don't have to go up so much anymore. But he was like firecracker. Sometimes, he would get really mad and explode."

"Did he have a steady girlfriend?"

He smiled. "He had many women."

"Any in particular when you worked in Fort Myers?"

"Like I say, he was good with girls. I don't know no names, just that he had a lot."

"What about family?"

"He had sister in Orlando. I remember he went there. He said she was very sick."

Holy shit. Why didn't I check Facebook? I knew Eisner had used it, but it was two years since he'd posted anything. I'd bet clues to his sister and a couple of his former girlfriends would be there.

"Was his sister married?"

"I don't know."

"Here's my card. If you hear from Barry, call me right away. And don't tell him I'm looking for him."

Chapter 46

Juan Espeza had the look of a Christian standing in the middle of the Colosseum seconds before the lions rushed in. He was pacing in interview room number three. No matter what I said to him, I was sure he thought he was about to be arrested or deported.

Captain Morales came down the hallway. I'd asked him to speak with Espeza, in Spanish, to assure him we only wanted his help.

Morales greeted Espeza and had him take a seat. I didn't understand what he said, but Espeza seemed a bit more at ease. By the way he used his hands, Morales appeared to be explaining the photo lineup process. Espeza nodded, and Morales smiled, raised a finger, and left the room, saying to me, "He may not shit his drawers, but he's still nervous."

"I feel bad for him."

"Why don't you let me administer the lineup? He seems to trust me. I'll do it in English and in Spanish."

I handed him the file with the consent forms and photos. "Sure."

"I'll grab him a Coke, and then we'll do it."

Morales handed Espeza the soda, and I listened to him ask our witness in two languages if he had been pressured. Then Morales explained he was going to show him two sets of six photos, one picture at a time, to see if he could recognize any of the men as the one he saw arguing with Jillian Evans.

Espeza nodded, and Morales set the first picture on the table. The landscaper shook his head after five seconds. A second image was put on the table. It was Eisner. The landscaper hovered over it and picked it up.

He studied the picture, raising my hopes, before shrugging and putting it down.

He passed over the remaining four photos quickly. The only one he spent any time on was Eisner. It had to mean something.

Morales did the paperwork and chatted with Espeza before starting round two. He placed the first picture down, and Espeza shook his head. When the next one was laid down, Espeza quickly waved it off.

Morales replaced it with the third image. It was Jafar Kapur. I studied Espeza, he appeared to slightly nod as he looked at the photo. He said something in Spanish. Morales responded in Spanish, repeating it in English for the record. "He looks familiar to you?"

"Si."

"Is he the man you saw arguing with Jillian Evans inside the house you were working on?"

"I don't know."

That was as close as we came to getting an identification. Disappointing? Yes, but it wasn't a bust as far as I was concerned. The only two men Espeza spent any time looking at were Eisner and Kapur.

Chapter 47

George Evans promised to swing by the office before eleven. I'd told him I needed to speak to him about a suspect. It was technically true, but I didn't care if he felt I'd brought him in under false pretenses. I was getting tired of his evasiveness.

Derrick brought him into our office and said something about an appointment. I didn't want Evans to feel outnumbered. His "I just ate a lemon" look and dull color made me wonder how the hell Jillian fell for him. Then I remembered the problems she had. Maybe this guy gave her a sense of stability, something she needed. It certainly wasn't his looks or demeanor.

His gray shirt looked fresh. He'd either changed before coming or wasn't out in the field today.

"Thanks for coming by."

"No problem. I have to check on a job down this way anyway."

"Where are you working?"

"We're putting a couple of new units on the Synovus Bank building."

"The ugly building on Forty-One?"

"Yep. It used to be a jewelry exchange, I think."

"It's been a while, but I think you're right. You want something to drink?"

"No."

"The last time we talked, you got pretty upset at the news that Jillian was pregnant and that it seems you were the father."

"It surprised me."

"You didn't know?"

He shook his head.

"Do you think she could have asked you to come over to tell you that she was pregnant?"

"Maybe. I don't know."

"Do you know Barry Eisner?"

Evans blinked. "Who?"

"You heard me. Barry Eisner."

"I, I don't know. It sounds familiar, but I'm not sure."

"Would it help if I told you that your wife had dated him?"

His shoulders slumped. "What do you want me to say?"

"Who did you hire to replace the roof on your home?"

"My roof? What does that have to do with Jill's death?"

"You hired Murphy's Roofing, right?"

"Yeah, so what?"

"Barry Eisner works for them. He was the supervisor on your job." I slid a picture of Eisner across my desk. "This jog your memory?"

"Oh, yeah, I remember him. But what's this got to do with anything?"

"Eisner is a suspect in Jillian's murder."

"Oh my God. Really?"

Something was off with this guy. His body language didn't match his vocal patterns. "Yeah, really, and he's disappeared. You know where he might have gone?"

His upper lip glistened. "Me. How would I know?"

"You knew him. Maybe you hired him to kill your wife."

"Why would I do that?"

It wasn't an outright denial. "I'm the one asking the questions here. How well did you know Barry Eisner?"

"I hardly knew him."

"That's not what his coworkers said."

"Who said what?"

"Unfortunately, I'm not allowed to reveal that information."

"Well, whoever said it was lying."

He was guarded, and I had nothing concrete. I danced a little more with him and let him go. When I caught up with Eisner, I'd see what he had to say about knowing Evans. Though remote, there was a chance they killed her together.

I sent a text to Derrick that the interview was over and went back to piecing Eisner's Facebook contacts together. Looking at pictures of the women on Eisner's page, I ran into one who bore a resemblance to Eisner. Her name was Betty Williams. Could it be the sister?

I wanted to see whether she was from Orlando, but Derrick stormed into the office. He stopped in front of my desk.

"You're never going to believe it."

Here we go again. "Believe what?"

"Just got off the phone with a Miranda Tessor. She dated Jafar, like two years ago. Said he was a lunatic and a liar. He pinned her down one night and slapped her in the face."

I jumped up. "Are you fucking kidding me? We got another goddamn coward on our hands? I'll strangle that punk myself."

"Take it easy."

"Find out where this bastard is. I want to go talk to him."

***

I sped along Old 41 and turned into Spanish Wells. Jafar Kapur was working from home today. His house was a one-story, Mediterranean-styled place surrounded by heavy vegetation. Was he a private man or one with something to hide?

He answered the door in linen pants that were so heavily wrinkled they reminded me of an accordion. He was shoeless but wearing socks that looked like gloves for your feet. Just looking at them made me wiggle my toes. They looked uncomfortable as hell. Who created those and why?

"Detective Luca, come on in."

There were curved walls and arched doorways but not much furniture. We headed past the kitchen into the family room. The cathedral-ceilinged room had two large TVs, an exercise bike, and a rowing machine. This guy's ideas on relaxing were from another planet. I wanted to live long, but if this was what it would look like, I'd have to reconsider.

"Have a seat. I'm going to grab a drink. Would you like something?"

"No."

He went into the kitchen, and my eyes swept the place, freezing when I saw a huge glass tank with a pink hue. It looked like a fish tank, but getting closer, it contained a large blue iguana.

Jafar was holding a bottle of something the color of swamp water. "You getting to know Dexter?"

"I've never seen a blue one before."

"They're from the Cayman Islands and nearly extinct. But what's interesting is they're the longest-living lizards on the planet."

"You're studying it?"

He unscrewed the cap of his drink and took a sip. "Not Dexter, specifically, but their diet, which is plant based, is something we find over and over with longer-living species."

"Really?"

"What's fascinating about the blue iguana is the way they handle the osmoregulation."

"Osmo what?"

"Plant matter contains more potassium and less nutritional content than other foods and thus must be consumed in larger quantities to meet the lizard's metabolic needs. This creates excess salt and potassium that must be disposed of. These lizards developed a lateral nasal gland to supplement its excretion of potassium and salt."

I didn't like this guy, but he was a fascinating person to listen to. "Are you saying that through evolution these iguanas developed a new gland?"

"We believe so. Unfortunately, we don't have infallible proof, but studies of skeletal fragments point that way."

"That would mean they changed their diets, then."

"Ah, very good, Detective. There are many theories, but I've never explored them myself. It would be interesting to know the whys, but my focus is on longevity."

He was interested in prolonging life, and I was trying to find out who had shortened the life of Jillian Evans.

I followed him into the family room, asking, "You work from home often?"

"Not particularly. When I want to do some thinking, it helps not to have distractions. These are complex problems, and not all of them can be solved hovering over a microscope."

We took seats opposite each other.

"I understand your father was a violent man."

He took a gulp of his concoction and slowly screwed the cap on. "You could say that, and it would be accurate. However, and I'm not defending him, we mustn't forget that he was from another place and time."

"Where killing your sister is normal?"

"No, of course not. I lost my beloved sister. We were very close. It was tragic."

"But you think his actions were justified?"

"Absolutely not. I'm simply saying it is a good deal more complicated than what it appears."

I wanted to choke his ass to get him to say what he was dancing around. "I assume you're referring to protecting the honor of the family."

"Yes, it seems archaic, but that was the world he grew up in. It's not something I subscribe to."

"It looks like you're more like your father than you realize."

"Excuse me?"

"Miranda Tessor."

He fiddled with the cap. "What about her?"

"You were physical with her. You pinned her down and slapped her."

"She deserved it."

I took a deep breath. "Deserved it? That's bullshit. In my book, no woman deserves being abused. They annoy you, you walk away."

"Let me explain. Our relationship was petering out, and I'd started to date another woman. It was someone she knew, actually, one of her friends. One night she came over unannounced, and I was with this other lady. As you can imagine, Miranda was upset. It was rather embarrassing for her friend, who left when Miranda went into a rage. There was no calming her down."

"So, you hit her?"

"She struck me first. I was simply trying to stop her from hitting me and throwing things at me."

Whether he was telling the truth would come out soon. It may not have been as bad as I originally thought, but it was evident he'd been physical with a female.

Chapter 48

Jessie loved going grocery shopping with us. She especially liked the kid carts that Publix had. I pushed her down the cereal aisle.

"Which one you want, Jess?"

I picked up a box of Fruity Pebbles and one of Chex.

"That's the fourth box, Frank. You can't get everything she points at."

"She likes these. Right, Jessie?"

She smiled, and I put both boxes in the cart.

"You're ridiculous. Go grab some milk. We're gonna get olive oil and some soups."

I grabbed a low-fat and an almond milk and found them in the pasta aisle talking to someone who looked familiar. It was the woman with all the piercings I'd seen at Jafar's office.

She said, "Your daughter is one bundle of joy. She's so happy."

"Thanks. I remember you from Xtended Living. I was there the other day, but I guess you went to that conference."

"Conference? I don't know anything about that. A bunch of us were laid off."

"Really? I thought business was good."

"More hype than reality."

"What do you mean?"

"I have to run. My mom is in the checkout line already, and I just came to get this." She held up a box of bow-tie pasta.

Groceries loaded up our cart as I chewed over why Jafar had lied. Was he simply embarrassed by having to reduce his workforce, or was he covering up the fact his business was failing? Was this evidence of a pattern of lying?

***

If I wasn't thinking about the Evans murder, I was contemplating ways to make sure Jessie didn't fall prey to an abusive man. Mary Ann thought I was overreacting, and each time I brought up the subject she'd pacify me. Half of me felt she might be right, but who would take fifty-fifty odds with their kid?

Sleeping was getting to be a problem. I'd nod out quickly, usually watching shows that were either boring or ridiculous, and go to bed around eleven. It would only take fifteen minutes to fall asleep if I was able to blank out any negative thoughts. The problem was I'd usually wake up around two, unable to go back to sleep.

That was the time when I found it impossible to shut down my thoughts. Invariably, I'd worry about protecting Jessie. Kicking around how to keep her safe, and whether I'd be able to detect signs of a developing problem almost guaranteed I'd lie awake for two hours. Last night was no different, but I had an idea that I thought could work.

Pulling into the parking lot for Rupert's Karate Academy, I saw a mother holding hands with a kid in a white robe. As they closed in on the entrance, the kid shook off his mom's hand and pulled the door open. He was taking the lead; I liked that.

The noisy lobby of the academy was filled with chattering kids and parents talking over them. There were only three girls among the dozen robe-clad kids. A teenager came out of a back room and said, "Sensei is ready to receive you."

At the mention of the instructor, the kids went quiet. The parents stopped chatting as their kids lined up. An impressive show of respect.

The teen bowed slightly, turned around and headed into the studio with the line of students in tow. A forty-something instructor with a lean but muscular build greeted each child with a deep bow.

He demonstrated how to deflect someone lunging toward you, using the teen as a proxy for an attacker. Leaning away, he extended his arm, placing it on the teen's shoulder and using the teenager's momentum, pushed him past, using his foot to send him onto a mat.

I wondered how I'd do against someone like him. It'd been years since I'd taken a slew of courses in self-defense. They were worthwhile, but most of us had come to rely on brute strength and our weapons.

The kids paired up, and the instructors had them emulate the move. I focused on the girls. They seemed to be performing the maneuver as clumsily as the boys were. Most times both kids would end up in a tangle on the floor.

It was cute, not intimidating, but unquestionably equalizing. I could see the value in a female removing the physical fear of a male. And if some of them could learn how to deliver a blow to an aggressive male, I was all in.

Karate or another kind of martial arts was something Jessie was going to learn. At worst, it provided structure and exercise. Plus, the kids seemed to embody a type of respect not found in a dance class or a ball field.

I had a slice of time to kill before talking to someone I was itching to. Using the space to come here was what I loved to do, optimizing the time I had. I grabbed a handful of literature along with an application and left. Back in the Cherokee, I headed to see Jafar's old girlfriend.

Hearing two versions of what had happened was as common as seeing cars stopped at a red light. My job was to tease out the truth. Well, the reality was to get as close as possible to what had occurred.

It was just before four, and the Fifth Avenue dinner crowd hadn't yet materialized. I parked alongside Truluck's Seafood Restaurant and went to see Miranda Tessor. Jafar's ex-girlfriend was a member of a long-time theatrical group known as the Naples Players. They were housed in the Sugden Theatre, anchoring a plaza filled with eateries.

I knew the group was building a large modern theater near Bayfront, but this place was impressive to me. Looking at a wall of posters with upcoming shows, I recalled their shows were critically acclaimed and made a mental note to take Mary Ann to one.

Miranda had told me to meet her outside of Blackburn Hall. She was rehearsing for *Bye Bye Birdie*, which was opening in under a week. As

I passed the box office, I noticed a woman sitting on a bench outside the entrance. She was moving her lips as she read.

The woman didn't raise her head until I was standing right in front of her. She had on those cat-eye glasses that women were favoring these days. Mary Ann said they gave your face a lift. I wasn't sure if it was another marketing gimmick.

"Miranda Tessor?"

She dropped the reading material getting up. "Uh, yes. That's me. You're the detective?"

"Yes, Detective Frank Luca."

Miranda bent down, picked up a handful of papers and dropped them as she reached for the others. I bent down to help, wondering how someone who performed on stage could be so nervous.

"I don't know what's gotten into me today. I flubbed a bunch of lines in the first act and then made my entrance in act two in the wrong scene."

"You said you open in a couple of days, right?"

She adjusted the pile of hair on her head as she stood. "Yeah, but I may not be in it."

"Why is that?"

"After today? The director was fuming at me."

I didn't know anything about acting, but there was no doubt she was a drama queen.

"I'm sure you'll be fine."

"You don't know this guy; he's a meanie. Nobody likes him."

"I realize you're busy. Let me ask my questions, so you can go back to rehearsing."

Tilting her head, she flashed her doe eyes at me. "Okay."

"You spoke with my partner, Detective Dickson, and told him about an incident with Jafar Kapur."

"Oh, I didn't know he was your partner. He was nice."

Did that mean I wasn't? "Tell me about Mr. Kapur."

"Well, we met at Food and Thought. It's a health food store. We were in the same aisle, and I grabbed a tub of hummus and put it in my basket when he said that I should try another brand, that it was better for me. It seemed pushy to me, but he compared the labels, and well, you know he's a health nut. Too much, if you ask me."

"How long were you dating?"

"About a year."

"How would you describe him?"

"A dreamer. Full of himself and arrogant. Whatever he wanted was all that mattered. As time went on, it became difficult for me to stay in the relationship."

"Mr. Kapur indicated that he was the one who ended it between the two of you."

"That's typical. He has a problem facing the truth."

"You told my partner that Mr. Kapur physically pinned you down and slapped you."

"Yes, that's correct."

"What transpired before the altercation?"

"We were arguing, and it just happened."

"Did you file a report of the incident?"

"No. I probably should have. My wrists were bruised. They hurt for days afterward."

"What were you arguing about?"

"We were always fighting. He was very stubborn."

"I understand that you caught him cheating with another woman. Was that what the fight was about?"

"I think it might have been."

"Wasn't the woman he was with a friend of yours?"

"What does that have to do with it? He threw me to the ground and slapped me. Then he held me down against my will. He wouldn't let me up. I don't know if it qualifies for kidnapping, but it's abuse of some kind, isn't it?"

"Yes. I'm not discounting what he did. All I'm trying to do is get context on the situation."

"What did he do anyway? Your partner wouldn't tell me."

"We don't know if he did anything. We're simply conducting a background check."

"It has to do with his business, right?"

I finished the interview uncertain of what I'd learned about Jafar Kapur. Had he gone too far by restraining her? She seemed like the type to go off, but whatever had happened didn't give him the right to slap her.

Chapter 49

I'd located a Betty Williams who was employed at the Bonefish Grill on International Boulevard in Orlando. The woman worked the noon-to-nine shift. I watched the clock hit eleven forty-five and picked up the phone.

The restaurant sounded as if it was in the midst of a Mother's Day brunch. One thing was sure about visitors to Orlando: if they weren't in one of the amusement parks, they were out eating.

A smoker's voice said, "This is Betty. Who's this?"

"Detective Luca. I'm with the Collier County Sheriff's Office."

"Collier County? That's Naples, ain't it?"

"Yes, ma'am."

"This have somethin' to do with Barry?"

As soon as she heard police, her mind went to her brother.

"Yes."

"What's he got himself into now?"

"I'm not sure it's anything, but he seems to have disappeared."

"Like, in you think he's dead?"

"We have no reason to believe that anything bad has happened to him. We're trying to track him down, so we can ask him a couple of questions."

"Uh-huh."

"Do you know where he is?"

"No idea."

"When was the last time you spoke to him?"

"I don't know. A coupla weeks ago."

"Did he say anything out of the ordinary?"

"Nah, he calls every now an' then to see how I'm doing. A coupla years ago I had a kidney transplant."

"Is there anyone who you think would be aware of his whereabouts?"

"We don't see much of each other anymore. But we're still blood, an' if I need somethin', Barry would be there for me."

I gave her my number and asked her to call me if she heard from him, but I knew she wouldn't. It was time to put out an all-points bulletin on Eisner.

***

As soon as I got back to the office, I had Derrick draft an APB. Though we were uncertain if he owned a firearm, it was protocol to mention that he was considered dangerous. We didn't have enough to consider going public and kept the distribution with the Collier and Lee sheriff departments.

I reviewed the APB request, and it was perfect. "Good job. Do me a favor, and take this upstairs."

My plan was to give it two days before going statewide with the alert. If he didn't show up a week after that, we'd ask the public for help in finding Eisner. I wasn't sure what was worse: waiting for someone to find him or that I was relying on someone else.

I updated the case file with notes on what Eisner's sister had said and realized I hadn't done that for my chat with Jafar's girlfriend, Miranda Tessor. After recording the info, I thought about what the woman in the grocery store had said about her former employer and picked up the phone.

"Mr. Kapur, this is Detective Luca."

"Oh, hello, Detective. How are you?"

"Good. I have a quick question."

"Okay."

"The other day, when I came to your office, I mentioned that there seemed to be fewer people working than the first time I'd been there. You told me that was because your people were attending a conference."

"I don't remember exactly, but I think that was right."

"What conference was that?"

"Uhm, there are so many of them, I don't recall."

"Try harder. It was only two days ago."

He paused. "Well, to tell you the truth, it's rather a delicate subject."

So, you were lying all the other times? "Facts may be uncomfortable, but they're not delicate. Tell me what's going on."

"We had a minor issue with one of the firm's contracts. It's a temporary situation, and we're currently working on a renewal. In the meantime, we had to furlough some of our colleagues."

Was this guy a techie or a lawyer? "You laid off staff?"

"Temporarily."

"Why did you lie about it?"

"I trust you can understand how critical our image is at this stage. If people believed we were in trouble, and we're not, by any means, they wouldn't support us."

"So, you lied to an officer of the court about it?"

"I, I didn't mean anything by it. It has nothing to do with what happened to Jill."

He was right; it wasn't about his girlfriend. It was all about the type of person he was. The other thing that bothered me was his choice of words to describe her murder. Was that an attempt to lessen the act that he had committed or simply human nature that sought to soften emotions at the loss of a loved one?

After hanging up, I went back to the case file and read the notes from my first meeting with Jafar. The foot soldiers who spoke with neighbors hadn't been able to verify the time he claimed to have left Jillian's home, but we were able to get a Starbucks barista to say he was in for his coffee that morning.

"We need to double- and triple-check everything. We know Eisner lied about his alibi. Evans was there but claims to have found his ex dead already, but what about Jafar?"

"The kid at Starbucks said he was in that morning, like he said."

"Yeah, but memories aren't reliable, especially when we're talking about the mundane and ordinary. The day-to-day stuff in life isn't as firm as you think. Unless there's an anchoring event that sears it into your memory, it's fuzzy for everyone."

"You're right. I can still see everything when the terrorists attacked the Trade Center. It's like time froze."

"Me too. And the days after, it was a mess up in Jersey. Everything came to a halt. People were walking around shell shocked."

"Those frigging bastards."

"Why don't we grab whatever CCTV Starbucks has of the morning of the murder. The kid said Jafar was in for his coffee, and maybe he was. You never know what we can get from it. Jafar might have been with someone or was acting weird."

"Sure. I'll ask Mac to send a uniform to grab the video."

I thumbed through the crime scene photos. Gianelli had taken a slew of close-ups of the bruises on her neck. Jafar was missing the tip of his forefinger. If he had strangled her, it could leave a telltale sign. I studied the photos. They looked normal to my eye, but I didn't have the experience Bilotti had.

The forensics lab said that Bilotti was out teaching a class at Gulf Coast University. I sent him an email regarding Jafar's forefinger and was about to call Mary Ann when Derrick rushed into the office.

"Guess who knew about the pregnancy?"

It was such important information that I let the guessing game slide. "Had to be Evans."

"Yep. His brother said that George told him Jillian was pregnant in a phone call. He thinks it was a couple of days before she was killed."

"Check the phone records. I want to know exactly when they spoke."

"You think she might have told him that she was going to get an abortion and he lost it?"

"Could be, or she could have told it him it was Jafar's, and he flipped out."

"Why would he lie about it, if it wasn't something he wanted to hide?"

"Let's assume he killed her. He went there to talk to her, and she sprang either aborting it or that Jafar had fathered the baby. He couldn't deal with it and strangled her. He must have known we'd find out during an autopsy, so his choices were to let us know he was the father, using the information to bolster his innocence."

"But he chooses to try and hide it. How could he have known we wouldn't be able to test the DNA of the fetus?"

"There's no way he'd know that. He decided to play dumb, that's it. Nothing else makes sense, other than saying he knew and would never harm his baby."

"Unless he knew he wasn't the father, or he thought he wasn't."

"It's weird. Lying about it makes him look bad and doesn't do anything to make him less of a suspect."

The phone rang, and Derrick picked it up. A second later he was on his feet and hung up.

"They got eyes on Eisner. He's fishing off the pier on Fifth Avenue."

"Let's get going."

Chapter 50

The Naples Pier was in the downtown area and a popular spot for tourists to visit. Built in 1888, it was originally a passenger and freight pier bringing visitors and supplies into the area. The pier played a critical role in the development of Naples and had been recently upgraded. It was a gathering spot for watching sunsets and to fish.

We parked just past Palm Cottage, the oldest home in Naples, and walked to the pier. I noticed one of our undercover guys. He had a line in the water and a bucket by his feet. We strolled by him, passing the concession and restroom facilities, toward the end of the pier.

Fishing off the southern side was Barry Eisner. He was wearing white cutoffs and a beat-up safari hat. His back to us, I said, "Catching anything, Mr. Eisner?"

He swung around. "What do you want?"

"Where have you been?"

He reeled in his line. "Key West."

"Hiding down there?"

"Nope, fishing. A buddy of mine has a boat. We hung out drinking brews and going out for tarpon."

He cast his line, and I said, "We need to talk to you. Take your line out, and come with us."

"Are you shitting me? This is bullshit, man."

Derrick stepped forward. "Take it easy, or we'll have to cuff you."

"Why can't you leave me the fuck alone?"

"We can do it the easy way or the hard way. It doesn't matter to me."

He muttered nonstop as he reeled his line in. Eisner wasn't going to resist. My next worry was whether he would insist on having a lawyer present during our interview.

***

Eisner was slumped in a chair waiting in interview room two. Since he was in shorts, it would take longer to raise the room temperature to an uncomfortable level. Call me childish, but it was something I always did, and it seemed to work. Though I was in a rush, I wasn't going to tempt fate.

Instead, I'd use the time to check my emails. The amount I received seemed to grow every day. As far as I was concerned, they fell into three categories: short and meaningless ones that people sent to acknowledge something; the cover-your-ass types, where someone would copy everyone they knew, and you'd have to waste time reading it all the way through to be sure there wasn't something you had to do; and the important ones.

Derrick found me in the cafeteria filling a cup with coffee.

"We got the Starbucks video, and guess what?"

I silently poured skim milk into my mug.

"Kapur was there, but not at the time he said he was."

"What?"

"Kapur said he left Jillian's house at eight and went to get a coffee before going to work. Well, according the time stamp on the video, he was there at nine forty-six."

"That's just before the first nine-one-one call. It doesn't make sense. George Evans had to see him, or vice versa. The timing is too close."

"I know, but he lied."

"We have to bat this around. Let's deal with Eisner first."

***

The thermometer read seventy-eight. Not optimal but respectable. Derrick saw me smile as I lowered it to seventy-two. He shook his head and knocked on the door.

We entered, feigning apologies for a mis-set thermostat, and took chairs.

As Derrick fiddled with the recording equipment, I said, "Look, I'm sorry we had to pull you away from fishing. We have a couple of questions that should clear things up. You'll be back on the water before you know it."

"I need a cigarette."

"Sorry, there's no smoking allowed in the building."

Derrick recited the formalities, and I held my breath when he came to the part about his right to have a lawyer present. Eisner didn't say anything. Was he going to remain quiet?

"Where were you the last couple of days?"

"I told you, in the Keys."

"You have somebody that can verify that?"

"Yeah, my buddy Mack. We were together, almost the whole time." He smiled. "Except when I was bagging a nice little piece of ass."

"Does Mack have a last name and address?"

"Porter's his last name. He's got a little place right by the Half Shell Raw Bar. Like, a block from Ferry Terminal."

"So, you just went down for a little vacation, then?"

"Yeah, that's right."

"The people at Murphy's Roofing didn't know about it."

"I ain't no slave to nobody."

"You could lose your job that way."

"Man, there's so many roofing jobs out there, I couldn't give a shit what they do. They fire me, I'd get another one like that." He snapped his fingers.

"The day that Jillian Evans was murdered you said that you were working in Briarwood."

"Yeah, I think that's right."

"You want to think that over?"

He picked at a nail. "Nah."

"Did you go anywhere else that morning?"

"I don't think so. I can't remember that good."

"Well, we have you on tape leaving Briarwood and entering Manor Care Health."

"Yeah, so what?"

"Manor Care is just behind the Evans house. And the time you were there lines up with when she was strangled to death."

"Hey, man, I didn't do anything."

"Murphy's Roofing said the roof you were working on at Manor Care was finished weeks ago. What were you doing there?"

He hesitated before smiling. "I was having a quick screw. Yeah, she was pretty sweet."

Was he making this up? "You left the Briarwood job site to have a sexual rendezvous with someone at Manor Care?"

"Yeah, that's right. You should try it; makes the rest of the day a lot better."

"If that was the case, why didn't you say something the first time we asked?"

He shrugged. "I was working. Didn't want them to know I left a job."

"But you just said roofing jobs are a dime a dozen."

"They are."

"So why couldn't you be straight?"

"What I can I tell you? It was just a quick lay."

"Who was the woman you claimed to have been with?"

"Eve Johnson."

"She works at Manor Care?"

"Yeah, she's an aide or something."

"And where did this sexual encounter take place."

Another hesitation. "In her car."

"What kind of a car does she have?"

"I don't know, a Honda or something."

"We're going to check this out."

"Can I go now?"

"You're going to have to stay until we verify this."

"That's bullshit, man. I want a lawyer."

We didn't have anything more than Eisner lying to us and him being close to Evans' house during the time she was killed. We'd have to arrest him to hold him.

"Take it easy. We'll release you, but you had better stick around town."

He stood and nodded.

"Wait here. I'll get someone to drive you back."

Before he left, I made sure we were going to have eyes on him twenty-four seven. If he tried to run for it, we'd haul him back in.

***

I hung up the phone. "What's with this case?"

Derrick said, "What did Manor Care say?"

"Eve Johnson went to Haiti, a family illness."

"Geez, what are the odds? Hey, you think Eisner knew that?"

"It's possible. She left five days ago. Make sure the surveillance on him is tight. He might take off."

"Okay. Is there a way we can get in touch with the family?"

"I asked them to check her file, but there was nothing in Haiti. We'll have to try to piece it together. I'm going to check and see if she's on Facebook."

"Make a request for her cell phone records, and check for Haitian numbers."

"I don't think a judge is going to sign off on that. But whatever happened with the call records on Evans?"

Derrick headed out of the office. "Let me check."

There were nine Eve Johnsons on Facebook. None appeared to be in the health field, nor were any of them living in Florida. I went to the DMV records. There was only one living in the area. I printed the record, dug deeper and grabbed her social security number.

When Derrick returned, he had a smile on his face and a single sheet of paper in his hand. "George Evans spoke to his brother around six p.m. on March second, less than three days from the murder."

"I still don't get it. Why lie about it?"

"I've been thinking about it, and I think she told him that she was going to get an abortion, and he freaked."

"I don't know. He's pro-life and wouldn't kill his own baby."

"Hold on a sec. He knew at least a couple of days before the murder that she was pregnant. He wants to get back with her, and in his mind, everything is perfect. They're together and going to have a baby. He had to be feeling pretty damn good. Then she turns on him, dropping a bomb that she's going to abort."

"She crushed his dreams, and he lashed out. Could be what happened. He's cracked under pressure before, hitting Jillian when his business was failing."

"Want to bring him in?"

"I'm afraid he's going to hire a mouthpiece and complicate things. Let me think this over. Right now, I'm leaning on calling him or catching him at work."

Chapter 51

I didn't want to alarm George Evans by showing up at his house or while he was working. Talking to a detective made even innocent people nervous, and Evans was a prime suspect in his wife's murder. I decided to call him in the evening, when he was home.

"Hello, George, it's Frank Luca. How are you?"

"Detective Luca?"

"Yes. How are you doing?"

"Okay. What's going on?"

"Not much, just a little thing I needed to clear up."

"Oh."

"You didn't know about Jillian's pregnancy. That's what I thought you said. Is that correct?"

"I don't remember exactly what I said. But I had a feeling she was pregnant."

"A feeling? What do you mean by that?"

"I knew her. Don't forget, we were married."

"Hold on a minute, she never told you she was pregnant, is that right?"

"I kind of figured it out on my own."

"How did you do that?"

"You know, she was nauseous a lot, and all of the sudden she wouldn't drink alcohol anymore, and Jill liked her vodka."

That could have tipped him off. "And when I asked you about it, you made like you had no idea."

"I didn't know for sure."

"So why did you say that you didn't know?"

"I don't know. I guess it would be embarrassing. She had other men in her life."

"But you told your brother that she was pregnant."

"He's family. He helped me a lot when she left the first time."

The first time? "Would you say you had a rocky marriage?"

"No, not at all. Things fell apart between us when my business went bad."

"That's when you hit her, when the pressure got to you."

"It was a bad time, and I regret it. There's nothing more I can say about it."

"I know that Jillian suffered from depression, which could make her behavior erratic at times."

"In the beginning it was a problem, but she was okay; really, she was."

"Would she leave and come back, when she wasn't feeling good?"

"No, she just left that one time."

"But you said earlier that your brother was helpful when Jillian left the first time."

He hesitated, then said, "I meant, you know, she left this time for good."

***

Unable to sleep more than four hours, I was grateful for the coffee Derrick had waiting.

"Morning, Frank."

"Morning."

"You talk to Evans last night?"

I hung up my jacket. "Yeah. He was tap-dancing like Fred Astaire. He said something that kept me up last night."

"What did he say?"

"He said his brother helped when Jillian left him the first time."

"The first time?"

"I let it go and circled back later. He seemed to backtrack, saying he meant that now she was gone for good."

"That's bullshit. It doesn't make sense."

"I know. All I could think of was her telling him, again, it was over right before she was murdered."

"Exactly. That jibes with what the girlfriend said; she was leaving Evans and Jafar for a fresh start."

I couldn't tell Derrick that Joyce had used fresh as well. "But even if she did, how do we prove he killed her?"

"He was at the scene. He called nine one one, with a huge gap in between calls. His DNA was on her. Evans knew she was pregnant with his baby. He called a criminal lawyer that morning. What else do we need?"

"We've got nothing but circumstantial evidence at this point. It's strong but circumstantial. We could get an arrest warrant, but a good lawyer would have no trouble winning in court, if it gets that far."

"You think so?"

"He's tricky, and we have him lying. He's not the best defendant, but unless we can get a witness to say they saw something or heard something, the case would be in trouble."

"But he slapped her and choked a guy who worked with him."

"Believe me, I know, but we need more."

"You know, we never showed that landscaper a picture of Evans. If we could get him to identify Evans as the man arguing with Jillian, we'd have something, right?"

"It would help. Still circumstantial, but I'll take it."

"Let me round him up."

"You know what? Get the pool tech back in. We might as well run a photo of Jafar past him."

***

My phone rang. It was Dr. Bilotti.

"Hey, Doc, how's it going?"

"Good, but it's going to get better in a couple of hours. I'm going to a tasting later at the Wine Cave."

"Sounds nice. What are they pouring?"

"Wines from Puglia, Italy."

"Puglia? I don't think I've ever had anything from there."

"You've probably heard of Bari. It's in Puglia, on the Adriatic Sea. The region extends all the way down to the heel of Italy. It's the second largest wine producing area in Italy."

"Wow. I better get cracking, then."

"If there's anything compelling tonight, I'll pick up a bottle for you."

"Thanks. Did you get my email?"

"As much as I like to talk about wine, it's why I called."

"Like I said, one of the persons of interest has a forefinger that's clipped. He's missing the top part. Is there any way to tell from the bruising whether the strangler might have been him?"

"During the initial examination, the bruising didn't reveal anything along those lines. I reexamined the photos, looking specifically for clues to asphyxiation by hand. It was an excellent idea, but I'm afraid that there was nothing inconsistent in the bruising pattern that would lead me to conclude the perpetrator's digits were compromised."

"Would you exclude this person of interest?"

"Tough to determine. If it was frontal pressure being exerted with the thumbs, which is likely, there may not have been enough force with the forefingers to leave a definitive mark."

That was the way Evans had choked his employee. "How would that be?"

"Bring your fingertips to your thumbs."

"Okay."

"You see it's natural for the thumb to touch your middle finger. That's where the strength in your hands lies."

How appropriate was that? The middle finger showing up in this case. The question was, who was flashing it at me?

Chapter 52

I made sure to get home a half hour before dinner to be with Jessie. My heart wasn't all the way into playing horsey with her. Tired from lack of sleep and distracted by the glacial pace of the case, I wanted to eat and read to her.

After making two trips around the cocktail table, I said, "Horsey needs a drink of water."

I carried Jessie into the kitchen, where Mary Ann was sprinkling garlic salt on a piece of fish. No pot on the stove top, meaning no pasta.

"That was quick."

"What else we having?"

"I made a salad, and there's a tray of broccoli in the fridge. Put it on the grill before you put the fish on."

I rolled my eyes.

"What's the matter?"

"I'm hungry. You get bread?"

"If you want to slim down you got to cut something, like carbs, or maybe you could stop drinking wine."

"All right, all right. I'll put the grill on."

After we ate, Mary Ann said, "Let's put Jessica in the stroller and go for a walk."

"Now?"

"You said you were going to walk every day. If you walk, you won't have to"—she fingered quotes—"starve yourself."

"I walked today."

"Yeah? How much?"

"I don't know, a lot."

"I'm going to get you one of those watches that tracks how many steps you take and your heart rate."

Just great. She'd check my stats every day and nag me if I didn't get enough activity.

"Don't be ridiculous. You want to go for a walk? Let's go."

***

Sending Captain Morales to retrieve Espeza was a good idea, but it didn't seem to work. The landscaper was as nervous as the first time we had him come in. As he paced the room, I worried that if we needed him to testify, he'd take off.

Speaking in Spanish, Morales put a hand on his shoulder and guided him to a seat. He must have said something funny, because Espeza flashed a gap-toothed grin. Before administering the photo lineup, Morales read the necessary protocols to the witness and laid the first picture on the table.

The gardener shook his head. Another image was laid down and dismissed quickly. The man in the third photo was George Evans. Espeza picked it up and brought it close to his face. I resisted the urge to burst into the room and ask if that was the man he saw arguing with Jillian.

He ran a hand through his hair and put the picture down. Morales asked if he was ready for the next one and Espeza nodded. After breezing through the final two pictures, Morales asked if he wanted to see them again.

My mind was screaming yes, but he shook his head no. Was this his way of removing himself from the case? Denying he could identify the man he saw arguing the morning of the murder made him useless to us. Even though someone must have told him that, and it was true, he seemed to signal something when he saw Evans' photo.

Was Espeza raging a mental battle between doing what was right against the fear the system would take over?

***

I nearly skipped down the hallway and into my office.

Derrick looked up from his monitor. "You win the lottery?"

"Not quite, but the pool tech said Jafar Kapur was the guy he saw in the back of the Evans house."

"Bingo, we got him."

"Not quite. Eyewitnesses are not only unreliable, but he wasn't at the house."

"What's next?"

"Draft a subpoena request for Kapur's phone records. I want to know who he called and where his phone was. We find cell towers by the murder scene pinging his phone, we've got something to corroborate the pool guy."

"You think we're going to get pushback from a judge on it?"

"No. Make sure you put in that we have an eyewitness who places him near the scene and that Jafar was in a relationship with the victim."

"I'm on it."

"If we get a hit, I'm going to open one of my only bottles of Saxum with you. Wait till you taste this stuff. You're going to love it."

"Sounds good. Hey, the case of wine you helped me pick out for the wedding came UPS yesterday. It was a good thing Lynn was home to sign for it; it was hot as hell yesterday."

"You have to be careful; you don't want your wine cooking in a UPS truck. It can get to a hundred and twenty inside a trailer."

As Derrick prepped the request, I called to check if Manor Care had heard from Eisner's love interest Eve Johnson. On hold, I was trying to recall the wines I had recommended to Derrick, when an idea hit me.

We needed to check the possibility that a UPS or FedEx driver had seen something that morning. Most times the drivers would rush to the door, drop a package, and hustle, eyes on their tablet, back to the truck. However, certain deliveries, like wine, required signatures. In those cases they'd have to ring the bell and wait. It had helped to catch two different killers in New Jersey. It was disappointing that I hadn't thought of it earlier. It could have been the chemo, but then again, Derrick hadn't thought of it either.

After Manor Care advised they hadn't heard from Eve Johnson, I spun my chair toward Derrick. "We need to find out what any UPS or FedEx drivers might have seen in Jillian's neighborhood the morning of the murder. Can you work on that? I'm going to Kapur's place of business and see about him being at work that morning."

"I'll check. They're always good at cooperating with general info."

Chapter 53

I tried to make sense of Jafar's claim that he was at work well before the murder occurred. The video coverage of the entrance of the building had Jafar entering and not leaving until lunchtime.

It didn't jibe with what the pool guy said or the footage from Starbucks. I drove around the building. There were two emergency exits that seemed to line up with Xtended Living's office. Signs were posted that they were alarmed and only to be used in an emergency. If he left through one of them, he'd have to have disabled them and avoided being seen.

It seemed unlikely. Driving back to the office, it looked like Starbucks' time stamp was off and the pool tech mistaken.

My mind shifted to Eisner and Evans. As I turned off Old 41, my cell rang. It was Derrick.

"What's going on?"

"Unless he's Houdini, it looks like Jafar was at work."

"Oh. Well, guess who's back in town?"

"The boys."

"What?"

"It was an old song: 'The Boys Are Back in Town.'"

"Oh. Eve Johnson came back from Haiti."

"How'd you know?"

"Manor Care called as soon as they heard from her. She called them from JFK. She's on a flight to Fort Myers tomorrow sometime and will be at work the following day."

The news was welcome. We were close to finding out if Eisner was lying or not.

***

My cell vibrated on the nightstand. It was 2:34 a.m. I answered, "Hello."

"Detective Luca?"

"Yeah. Who is this?"

"Officer Brown. We were doing the surveillance on Barry Eisner." Were? "And?"

"Well, we have a little problem."

"What the hell is going on?"

Jessie started crying, and I wanted to join her. Eisner had slipped out of the house and jumped in his vehicle. He must have gone out a rear window. No one noticed his pickup truck was missing until it was too late. It had been parked a couple of houses away.

It was going to be another long night. I put an APB out and headed to the office.

***

In addition to the APB, the department pulled a dozen officers out of their beds to hunt for Eisner. The effort was driven by their embarrassment. I felt for the officers who'd screwed up, but I was pissed they allowed Eisner to disappear.

I was too tired to go to the cafeteria for coffee. I closed my eyes for a second and felt my head bob as an email chimed in. It was from the AT&T legal department. It was Jafar's phone records.

I clicked open the PDF and perused through it, eyes about to close. On the morning of March fifth, Jafar Kapur's phone pinged two cell towers that straddled the area he lived in. It looked like he'd left his phone home. But he was at Jillian's that night. Did he go a whole day without his phone?

A techie without a phone? I heard it all. It seemed impossible. Then I remembered that article I read that the new thing for successful people was being out of touch. I couldn't think straight. I banged the desk with my fist.

"You okay?"

"No, I'm not! I'm frigging dead tired and can't think."

"You need a nap."

"Yeah, right. I'll nap on my desk like a five-year-old."

"Go out to your car. Put the air on. I'll come get you in twenty minutes. It's all you'll need."

I was too tired to think about it and trudged out to the Cherokee. I didn't even remember putting my head back. Next thing I knew, Derrick was knocking on the window. I felt like shit for a minute, but my head cleared, and I had some of my energy back. My first power nap.

Out of fear I'd slip, I grabbed a coffee from the cafeteria. I kept thinking over the phone records. It didn't make sense to me. I needed to see what Jafar would say about it. Either he'd clear it up or darken the cloud over his head.

"Jafar, this is Detective Luca."

"Hello, Detective, how are you?"

"I have a question for you."

"I have a meeting in five minutes."

"I'm curious about your phone."

"My phone? Oh, yeah, you noticed it's Apple's latest?"

"Do you take it with you everywhere?"

"Of course, who doesn't?"

"That's interesting, because on the morning that Jillian Evans was murdered, your phone was at your Spanish Wells house."

"You checked on the whereabouts of my phone?"

"It's standard operating procedure in a homicide case."

"But why my phone?"

"You were close to the victim."

"We were in a relationship, Detective. However, that does not give you a right to my personal information."

"A judge gave me the right. You said you left Jillian's home around eight a.m. and went for a coffee before going to work."

"That's right."

"How did your phone end up at your home?"

"I stopped off at my house to get changed and forgot it there."

"How come you didn't go back to get it? You must have realized that you left it behind."

"I didn't realize it until after I arrived at the office."

"But you live so close; why not go back for it?"

"I had a busy day."

"You also said that you walk to work from your home. Didn't you?"

"When I'm able to, I use my commute as exercise, provided my schedule and the weather permit me to."

"Fair enough, Mr. Kapur. I hope you understand why we had to investigate the inconsistencies in your statements."

"Of course, Detective. Though I detest the invasion of privacy and the insinuation it portrays, I understand you're just doing your job."

"I appreciate that, Mr. Kapur. Sorry to have interrupted you."

There was nothing to be gained by telling him the pool technician had identified him as the man he saw the morning of the killing. It could have been a case of mistaken identity, and I wanted to avoid putting Jafar on guard.

Chapter 54

I was elated they'd picked up Eisner on Marco Island. But my relief morphed into puzzlement. A patrolman found Eisner surf fishing on Tigertail Beach. He didn't try to run or resist, saying he was fishing for pompano.

We had to decide whether to arrest him or not. He was a murder suspect but hadn't done anything since we had eyes on him. Was his decision to run connected to Eve Johnson's return? It was a hell of a coincidence, and you know how I feel about them.

If he was running because his alibi wasn't going to hold up, why go fishing? I was expecting rationality, but I was operating in an irrational world with a sector of the population that made haphazard decisions.

The safe thing to do was to hold him, and I wanted to. The problem was Sheriff Chester wasn't on board. He had taken a bunch of heat once for the arrest of a man accused of rape. It was a hasty move, involving a teenager who'd been the homecoming queen. The accused man had known the girl and had given her a ride a couple of hours beforehand. As it turned out, the girl had consensual sex with a football player she had an unreturned crush on, reporting it as a rape.

The press beat up the sheriff for rushing to arrest a man who, though considered an oddball, was as innocent as the family dog. Given the torment of my first case, where a rush to arrest led to a teenage suicide, I agreed with being cautious. However, what was driving this wasn't prudence but politics.

Chester assigned a team of veterans to watch Eisner, assuring me he wouldn't slip away again. Given the embarrassment if Eisner did, I believed he'd be around if his alibi failed to check out.

***

I chuckled when George Evans jumped at the sound of thunder. A Hollywood director couldn't have staged the setting any better. A storm had rolled in just as Evans had arrived, and the interview room temperature had settled at a toasty seventy-nine degrees.

It was showtime. I knocked on the door and entered. "Mr. Evans, thank you for coming in. Geez, it's hot in here. Sorry about that, the unit is broken."

I hit record and cited the formalities, assuring him the recording was for his protection.

"I think I should get a lawyer."

"That's your right. You can wait here until whoever you get arrives, or we can proceed until then. I just have a couple of questions. It really shouldn't take long, if you'd like to cooperate."

"Okay, I'll cooperate."

"I want to review the morning of March fifth with you, when you went to your ex-wife's home."

Sweat trickled past his sideburn. "But we've been over this a hundred times."

"I know we covered this, but some new information has come to light, and I'd like to get your take on it."

His pasty face tightened. "What new information?"

"We have a witness who saw you arguing with Jillian the morning she was murdered."

"Who said that?"

Interesting that he asked who said it and not that it was impossible, since she was dead when he arrived.

"Never mind who said it. We know the witness was there that morning."

His shirt darkened by his armpits. "I don't get it. Wait a minute, is it that creep Jafar? Is he trying to frame me?"

"No. The person who observed the argument has no motive. In fact, they were reluctant to participate."

"Well, whoever it was is wrong."

"You were at her house that morning."

"Yes, I told you that."

"Why were you there?"

He sighed. "I told you, she called me to come over."

"Why?"

"She said she had something to tell me."

"And when she told you, it upset you, and you got into an argument."

"No. I didn't."

"And you lost control, strangling her to death."

His hands were trembling. "No. I didn't do anything. I told you she was dead when I got there."

"Come on, George, admit it. You killed Jillian Evans."

"I want a lawyer."

It was inevitable that he'd hire a mouthpiece. We were closing in, but all we had was circumstantial. He was there. He claimed to discover her dead when he arrived, but a witness saw him arguing with her. We knew she was ending the restart of her relationship with him. She was pregnant with his child, and the news could have tipped him over the edge.

***

It might have been the long day of travel, but Eve Johnson, dressed in a pink sweat suit, was nothing to look at. I don't know what I was expecting, but it wasn't her. Johnson was five feet, a hundred and twenty pounds, half of it in her rear.

Her soft-spoken demeanor was at odds with having sex on the job and in a car. Eisner was a good-looker, but he got around in a ten-year-old pickup, not a white horse. Maybe I was getting too old for this job.

"Ms. Johnson, I understand you just came back from Haiti."

"Yes, my grandmama is very sick."

"I'm sorry to hear that. I wanted to ask you about Barry Eisner."

"Barry? Did he do something?"

"Not necessarily. Mr. Eisner used you as an alibi."

Her eyes widened. "Me?"

"Yes. When was the last time you spoke to him?"

"Uh, a few days before I went to Haiti."

"Were you in a relationship with Mr. Eisner?"

She nodded.

"I'm going to ask you some personal questions. It's extremely important that you answer honestly. Lying to me or any other officer of the court could amount to obstruction of justice and subject you to a possible prison term. Do you understand?"

Her Adam's apple bobbed. "Yes. Don't worry, I'll tell the truth."

"On the morning of March fifth, did you meet up with Barry Eisner?"

"March fifth? I, I don't remember that date."

"It was the day the woman was murdered on the block behind Manor Care."

"Oh, yes. Now I remember. Barry came in the morning to see me."

"Where did you meet him?"

"Outside, in the back."

"And what did you do?"

"We, we talked."

"Did you go to your car?"

She looked at her feet and nodded.

"Did you and Mr. Eisner get in your vehicle and have a sexual encounter?"

I strained to hear her say yes.

"After it was over, what did you do?"

"I went back to work and Barry left."

"Did you see him leave?"

"Yes, he went out the side exit."

It looked like Eisner was off the hook. However, I wasn't going to call off the surveillance just yet. We knew nothing about Eve Johnson and whether she could be lying to protect him. People did the stupidest things for love and money, and lying was an easy one to rationalize. I could see her trying to weasel her way out, claiming I twisted what she had told me.

Chapter 55

I wondered how Corey Roberts managed heavier packages. His thin arms poked out of a brown UPS shirt, matching a body that looked like it belonged to a ten-year-old. Box in one hand, he pulled down the door to his truck with his other.

"Corey Roberts?"

He moved to the sidewalk. "Yeah, what's up?"

I flashed a badge. "Just a couple of questions."

He froze.

"You have nothing to worry about."

"I didn't think so, but you scared me. Hold on a second."

Roberts sprinted up a walkway, dropped the package, pulled out a handheld and tapped it before jogging back. "Thanks. I got a busy one today."

"I'll get right to it. You were in Lely Palms the morning a woman was murdered."

"Yeah, I remember hearing about it. I didn't know her though."

"That morning, March fifth, did you see anyone or anything unusual?"

"You know, I did. I had a delivery that needed a signature. I think it was from Apple."

"So, you'd have a record, with a time stamp."

"Oh yeah. You can get it from the office."

"What did you see?"

"I rang the bell and was waiting, and when I heard the AC compressor go on, I looked toward it and saw a man running, not running really, but in a hurry, you know what I mean?"

"Yes. How did you see this if you were at the front door?"

"It was one of those houses where the front door is to the side and set back."

It was one of my least favorite layouts. "Can you describe the man you saw?"

"He was kind of skinny and medium height. I didn't get the greatest look at him."

I pulled out photos of Eisner, Evans, and Kapur. "Was it any of these men?"

His eyes flashed recognition as he reached for one of the pictures. "I think it was him."

***

The smart move was to bring him in; see what we could get out of an interview. I was hoping he'd come alone, but deep down, I knew he wouldn't. I peered through the window, wondering if the inability to screw with the temperature would be a curse.

I took a deep breath and nodded at Derrick. He knocked and swung open the door. Palm on the table, Jafar Kapur was drumming his fingers. It was his good hand. His lawyer was someone I didn't know, but by his suit, he was a tier below the four-hundred-dollar-an-hour snakes defending drug dealers.

I nodded at Kapur and turned to his counsel. "Detective Frank Luca." I extended my hand. "This is Detective Dickson."

"Sherby Clauson."

Derrick shook hands, hit record, and stated the formalities of the interview.

"Mr. Kapur, where were you the morning of March fifth, 2019?"

His attorney nodded, and Kapur said, "I left Jill Evans' home at approximately eight a.m. I stopped for my customary coffee at Starbucks and went to work."

"I thought you went home first."

"Oh, sorry. I stopped at my home to change clothes and ended up leaving my phone behind."

"Did you leave your office that morning?"

"My private office?"

He was being a smart-ass. "No, your place of business."

"No. I remember having a full schedule that day. We were swamped."

"Were you busy because you laid off a bunch of staff?"

Clauson put his hand on Kapur's arm and said, "My client's business has nothing to do with the matter at hand."

"True to a degree, Counselor. Your client lied to me about the state of his business. But I'll move on. Are you certain about that?"

"Yes."

"We have an eyewitness who saw you behind Jill Evans' house that morning at a time that coincides with her time of death."

Clauson said, "Detective Luca, eyewitnesses are unreliable in general and particularly when trying to pinpoint a time."

"We're certain of the time, Counselor. The witness is a deliveryman, and the package he delivered was signed for, triggering an automatic recording of the time."

"No system is infallible."

"Mr. Kapur, you were granted asylum in the United States because your father, who is violent, killed your sister. Is that correct?"

"Yes."

"How did he kill her?"

"He choked her."

"The apple doesn't fall too far from the tree, does it?"

Clauson said, "That's unnecessary, Detective. Mr. Kapur came here freely to try to answer your questions, not to be harassed."

"I apologize. It was out of line."

"Apology accepted."

"Let me tell you what I think happened. You left Jill that morning, angry that she was carrying the child of her former husband and was going to end your relationship. You left, went to your house to leave your phone so there'd be no trail, then you went through the preserve to her house, where you strangled her to death."

"You have a vivid imagination."

"Your DNA was on her body."

"My client slept in the same bed as her the night before."

"Did you kill Jillian Evans?"

"No."

"I think you're lying."

"My client has told you he didn't do it. If you have more evidence than an eyewitness who merely purports to put my client in the vicinity, then present it. Otherwise, this interview is over."

Clauson stood up, and Kapur followed him, putting his hand on the table as he rose. That's when an idea hit me. Derrick said, "You'll go when we dismiss you."

I said, "It's okay. You can go."

Chapter 56

"Why did you let him go? It's him. I can feel it."

"We need more. But I have an idea that might prove he was there."

"What?"

"He was wearing a Fitbit."

"Yeah, a lot of people do."

"I know. Mary Ann is threatening to make me wear one to track how much exercise I get."

"What's your idea?"

"They use GPS to measure your steps, and that would leave a geographic footprint of his whereabouts."

"Oh man, the techie thought he was smart by leaving his phone home, but he forgot about the Fitbit."

"At least that's what I'm hoping. But we'll need a warrant to get access to his account and historical data. In the meantime, let's stay on Evans. If we can somehow corroborate what the landscaper thinks he saw—"

"Who else comes to your house? We have the landscapers, the pool guy. Maybe a tree service? Or what about some kind of meter reader, or someone from the county?"

"Go for it. We went over this already, but I'm all for making sure we didn't miss something. I'm going to write up the warrant request, then I'm going to dig into Eve Johnson. See what her background looks like."

***

The first place to check was the law enforcement touch database. Eve Johnson appeared four times, on the high side for a law-abiding citizen. Two were auto accidents, another was when she was a victim of a burglary, but what stood out was a perjury conviction.

I pulled up the case in question. A girlfriend of Eve Johnson's was on trial for stabbing a man. The woman claimed that the man was making unwanted sexual advances and that it was in self-defense.

Eve Johnson witnessed the stabbing and testified that the man was sexually aggressive, even making a pass at her. The accused had a witness who testified that the attacker was high on LSD, and produced phone video showing Johnson trying to calm the woman down before the stabbing.

The accused also had his doctor testify that his patient was taking Lexapro for depression and that the drug was known to suppress the sex drive. The judge dismissed the charges but charged Johnson with perjury.

She was lucky, avoiding a prison term, but was fined five thousand dollars and had to do thirty hours of community service. It was clear, Eve Johnson could not be trusted. We needed to apply pressure to see if she was covering for her lover.

***

We knew that George Evans called a criminal lawyer the morning of the murder. The timing of the call was a huge problem for the victim's ex-husband. Just minutes after the first 911 call, he dialed the number of Marshall Woodrow.

It made me sick that after disconnecting the first emergency call, he called for assistance, not for medical help for Jillian, but for legal advice.

Evans wanted us to believe he called the attorney for issues related to his failed business and had never spoken to Woodrow that morning. The more I thought about it, the more convinced I was that the call was critical to proving whether George Evans had murdered Jillian Evans.

The problem was the privacy protections governing attorney-client conversations. We couldn't compel an attorney to disclose the nature of a call. Was it really about his failed business?

I went to Woodrow's website to see if he handled business law. I rooted around his site, ending up on the contact page. The disclaimer on it caught my eye. It warned visitors looking for representation against leaving voice mails or sending emails with confidential information.

It hit me that Evans may not have been a client of Woodrow's. If he wasn't being represented by the lawyer, then attorney-client privilege didn't apply. The lawyer would be able to disclose if he spoke with Evans.

Calling Woodrow's office, I explained that I only wanted to know whether the firm was working for George Evans. They asked that the request be written, promising to answer the email as soon as possible.

I was now waiting on a second email to go along with the one from Fitbit. Instead of sitting around, it was time to press Eve Johnson. She'd perjured herself for a girlfriend. Was she doing it again?

Chapter 57

Derrick had his hand on the doorknob. "This was a long time coming."

"I would have liked to close it quicker, but the longer hunts are more satisfying."

"You ready?"

I raised the file I was carrying. "Yep, let's get this over with."

He swung the door open. Jafar Kapur and Clauson, his lawyer, stiffened as we entered.

"Mr. Kapur, Counselor. Thank you for coming in."

"I'm due in court in ninety minutes. I trust you'll extend consideration should this run longer than expected."

"No worries, Mr. Clauson. I don't expect this to take long."

Kapur's face relaxed but tightened again when Derrick stated the time and occupants.

I centered my file and said, "Mr. Kapur, your previous statements claim that you left Jillian Evans' home at around eight a.m. on March fifth."

"That's correct."

"You stated that you went to your home in Spanish Wells to change, leaving your phone behind, then you went to your office in the technology park on Old Forty-One."

"We've gone over this several times."

"Please bear with me. You stayed at your offices until lunchtime, around twelve fifteen."

"That's right."

"Based upon your statements, that would have put you far away from Jillian's home during the time period when she was strangled."

"Yes, I've told you I had nothing to do with it."

"That's a lie, Mr. Kapur."

Clauson leaned forward. "Excuse me, Detective, that's unnecessary."

I opened the file and took out two documents. "That's a matter of opinion, Counselor." Derrick smiled as I slid the documents across the table.

"What are these?"

Derrick said, "One has the coordinates and time stamps from your client's Fitbit device. The longitude and latitude readings detail his whereabouts on March fifth. The other is a map created with those coordinates. The red line represents your client's movements."

Clauson glanced at his client as Derrick continued.

"Mr. Kapur left the home of Jillian Evans at eight oh four and drove to his home, where he presumably dropped his phone. Then he went to his office, made an appearance, and backtracked, driving to Starbucks, where he parked. He then cut through the preserve, returning to her home at nine oh two. He had an argument with her and after strangling her to death, returned to his office."

I took a second copy of the map out and traced my finger over it. "You see here, this is you going back and forth through the woods."

"It wasn't me. I, I lent my Fitbit to a friend."

"And you gave him the keys to your house?"

"Yes. He went to feed my iguana."

"I'll give you an A for effort, Mr. Kapur, but we have you on Starbucks' video, corroborating the Fitbit data."

Clauson said, "We're going to need to authenticate these reports."

"You'll have to do that in a courtroom, Counselor. Stand up, Mr. Kapur. You're under arrest. Give me your hands." As I put cuffs on him, I said, "Read him his rights, Derrick."

Chapter 58

Before heading home, I needed to make one more call. I had already called George Evans. He was a suspect and an ex-husband as well. He deserved to know the news. It wasn't exactly protocol to call a victim's exes, but I also wanted Joyce to know we'd caught the killer, and the easiest way was to call her father.

"Hello."

It was Joyce. I thought of hanging up. "May I speak to Brian Wild, please."

"Sure, who's calling."

"Detective Luca from the Collier County Sheriff's Office."

"Oh, hi. This is Joyce."

"Hi, can I speak with your father?"

"You caught the person who did it?"

"Yes, but that's all I can say. May I speak with your father?"

"Thank you."

"What?"

"I said thank you. I'll get Dad."

When we needed a babysitter for Jessie in a couple of years, I hoped this kid would be interested in doing it.

***

"Where's Jessie?" I set a bottle of wine on the counter.

"Taking a nap. Celebrating the Evans case?"

"Bilotti gave it to me. He went to a tasting at the Cave."

"That was nice of him. So, how did Kapur react when you sprang it on him?"

"He tried to be cool, but you could tell he was mad. He thought he had everything planned, but even as smart as he is, he screwed up. I don't know if we would have pinned it on him without the Fitbit data."

"Did he confess?"

"No. I'm sure he's trying to find a way to explain it away. But we got a schematic of his offices. One of the emergency exits is right behind his office. Forensics will prove he disabled the alarm on it. All that's left is the nine-one-one call. But the more I think about it, it was probably him in a panic who made the first call. Either that or it was Jillian with her last breath, unable to complete the call."

"I wouldn't worry about it. The prosecutors will be able to give a plausible explanation to the jury."

"I'm not worried, just trying to understand how it went down. I'm going to get changed."

Mary Ann followed me into the bedroom. Jessie's dress was laid out on the bed. It was a mini wedding gown.

"I'm really looking forward to seeing how Jessie reacts with all the people at the church."

"She'll do fine."

"I wish she was a little older, so she could walk down the aisle like a real flower girl."

"She is a real flower girl."

"You know what I mean. The wedding's going to be a blast."

"Lynn's really happy the case is over. She was worried they'd have to postpone the honeymoon."

"They wouldn't have to do that."

"Derrick told her he didn't want to leave you alone with it."

"I told you he's a good guy. Makes me feel even better that he's Jessie's godfather. Anything happens to us, she's in good hands."

***

I was halfway through the bottle when my cell rang.

"Detective Luca?"

"Yes, who's this?"

"David McGregor. My wife and I were the victims of a robbery outside Cote d'Azur."

"Of course. How are you and your wife?"

"We're fine. I'm sorry to trouble you at this hour, but I wanted to let you know that we found my watch."

"It was misplaced, not stolen?"

"Oh no. My memory is going, but not that quickly. When it was stolen, I contacted Patek Philippe to let them know. They sent an alert out to all their authorized jewelers and repairmen to be on the lookout, and what do you know? Someone brought the watch in for an appraisal."

"That's fantastic news."

"You don't need it as evidence, do you?"

If he asked the prosecutors if they needed it, he'd never live long enough to see it. I felt his wife's watch was more than enough loss and evidence. "Don't worry about it. Give me the place who had it, and I'll establish a chain of custody for the watch."

"Excellent. I was afraid I'd have to part with it again."

"Glad to help you with that. Say hello to your wife for me."

Thank you for taking the time to read A Killer Missteps. If you enjoyed it, please consider telling a friend or posting a short review. Word of mouth is an author's best friend. Thank you, Dan

Dan has a monthly newsletter that features his writing, articles on Self Esteem & Confidence building, as well as educational pieces on wine. He also spotlights other author's books that are on sale.

Sign up - www.danpetrosini.com

Other Books by Dan

Luca Mystery Series

Am I the Killer—Book 1

Vanished—Book 2

The Serenity Murder—Book 3

Third Chances—Book 4

A Cold, Hard Case—Book 5

Cop or Killer?—Book 6

Silencing Salter—Book 7

A Killer Missteps—Book 8

Uncertain Stakes—Book 9

The Grandpa Killer—Book 10

Dangerous Revenge—Book 11

Where Are They—Book 12

Burried at the Lake—Book 13

The Preserve Killer—Book 14

Suspenseful Secrets

Cory's Dilemma—Book 1

Cory's Flight—Book 2

Cory's Shift—Book 3

Other works by Dan Petrosini

The Final Enemy

Complicit Witness

Push Back

Ambition Cliff